The Heart of a Savage

**Lock Down Publications &
Ca$h Presents**
*The Heart of a Savage
By Jibril Williams*

.

The Heart of a Savage

Lock Down Publications

P.O. Box 870494
Mesquite, Tx 75187

Visit our website at www.lockdownpublications.com

First Edition July 2019
Printed in the United States of America

This is a work of fiction. Names, characters, places, and incidents either are products of the author's imagination or are used fictitiously. Any similarity to actual events or locales or persons, living or dead, is entirely coincidental.

Cover design and layout by: Dynasty's Cover Me
Book interior design by: Shawn Walker
Edited by: Lauren Burton

Jibril Williams

Stay Connected with Us!

Text **LOCKDOWN** to 22828 to stay up-to-date with new releases, sneak peaks, contests and more…

Thank you!

Submission Guideline.

Submit the first three chapters of your completed manuscript to ldpsubmissions@gmail.com, subject line: Your book's title. The manuscript must be in a .doc file and sent as an attachment. Document should be in Times New Roman, double spaced and in size 12 font. Also, provide your synopsis and full contact information. If sending multiple submissions, they must each be in a separate email.

Have a story but no way to send it electronically? You can still submit to LDP/Ca$h Presents. Send in the first three chapters, written or typed, of your completed manuscript to:

LDP: Submissions Dept
Po Box 870494
Mesquite, Tx 75187

DO NOT send original manuscript. Must be a duplicate.

Provide your synopsis and a cover letter containing your full contact information.

Thanks for considering LDP and Ca$h Presents.

Dedication

I dedicate this book to every female who has been locked away in the struggle.

Please know, no matter what curveball life throws you, your value never decreases.

Acknowledgements

First, I want to acknowledge The Big Homie CASH and Shawn Walker for giving me the opportunity to experience this once-in-a-lifetime experience. Thank you both. The gesture will *never* be forgotten. *LDP for life!* That's real talk.

Big Salute to Jamaica. When I saw you personally acknowledge me in your book, *Blood Stains of a Shotta*, I felt that, and know a brother like me don't feel easily. Keep that pen to the pad and make it do what it do.

Much love to my biggest fans. LOL! There are so many of you. There's no me without you. You thought I didn't hear ya when you asked me to do something for the female readers, so here you go. This right here is for you. I hope you enjoy the ride.

Last, but not least, for my sister, Ashley. No matter what dream I pursue, you seem to always have my back and are ready to go H.A.M. about me at the drop of a dime. I love you, beautiful.

Get at me on Facebook: Jibril the Author Williams
Or follow me on Instagram: @Jibril

Jibril Williams

Chapter 1

"You bring out feelings in me I never show.
Nobody has made me feel dis way before.
I'm a good girl, but I wanna be bad for you,
I wanna be bad for you.
I wanna be bad for you,
Be bad, be bad, be bad for you."

Tata bounced and snapped her fingers as she sung along to the hook of Meek Mill and Nicki Minaj's song "Bad For You." As she grooved to the beat, she kept a close eye out for Rico and his team. This was the perfect theme song for the current situation. This song also truly expressed how she felt about Rico. She checked the face of her peach diamond Cartier watch. She knew at any moment Rico would be coming through the alleyway that sat across the street from the parking lot where she waited.

***

"Listen da fuck up! All I'm asking for is four fucking minutes of your time. You can use your brains to think with, or I can leave them splattered on the walls in this bitch," the robber said, wearing the rubber 2Pac mask as he walked into the jewelry store waving an MP-5 military-style weapon, which made the occupants of the jewelry store lock up in fear.

"Lay down! Lay face fuckin' down!" another robber said, sporting a Donald Trump mask. "I mean I don't want to see an eyeball in this bitch," he continued to shout.

It was fifteen people in total who picked the wrong day to shop at Boone & Sons Jewelers, located three blocks away from the Whitehouse on Pennsylvania Avenue.

"Three minutes," the 2Pac robber instructed his crew.

9

Another robber in a Jay-Z mask began breaking the glass of the six display cases with a mallet. The security at the store was weak and lacking much of the up-to-date technology the other jewelry stores had. Boone & Sons had cut corners with their security measures because they relied on the fact their establishment was so close to the Whitehouse with all its security and the constant police traffic that flowed past their store. No one was foolish enough to rob them. This flaw alone encouraged the robbers to hit this location.

2Pac stood in the middle of the store holding the MP-5, overseeing the hostages lying on the floor. Donald Trump followed behind Jay-Z, filling his black bag with the jewelry store valuables.

"Two minutes!" 2Pac called out, letting his partners know they had two minutes to grab everything they could from the display cases. Jay-Z had all the display glass smashed. He started helping Trump remove the store merchandise and place it in his own black bag.

Something caught 2Pac's attention. A white lady lay on the floor in front of him wearing a pencil dress. Her feet rocked a pair of open-toed, white Chanel sandals, and the middle toe of the lady's perfectly pedicured feet held an immaculate platinum, diamond-studded toe ring. The toe ring held six flawless princess-cut diamonds placed with perfection around the platinum band.

2Pac bent down, grabbed the woman's foot, and lifted it toward him. The movement slightly spread the woman's legs apart.

"Please, don't! I'll give you anything. I got money," the woman protested, bringing her hands down in front of her, covering her private area. The woman thought the robber wanted to rape her or get a cheap feel.

2Pac caught on to what the woman was insinuating. "Bitch,

please! Don't flatter yourself. Donald Trump is the one who grab pussy. I just grab the jewelry," 2Pac said, snatching the toe ring off the lady's foot and placing it in his pocket.

"One minute!" 2Pac yelled out. His team knew the drill too well. Calling the last minute meant they were out of the store, no matter if they had everything they came for or not.

"Done!" Jay-Z called out, letting 2Pac know all six display cases was empty.

"Time!" 2Pac shouted. "Let's go!"

Jay-Z and Donald Trump made their exit out of Boone & Sons Jewelers and got into the stolen Dodge van parked right out front of the store. 2Pac stood in the middle of the store, watching his hostage like a lion watches its prey. He heard the voice come through his earpiece: "All clear!" 2Pac then spun on his heels like a soldier, exited the store, and hopped in the back of the waiting van.

Jay-Z pulled the van from the curb and made a right on 14th and Pennsylvania Avenue. He pushed the van up two blocks, then quickly made a left into an alley. He snatched his mask off as Rico and Diesel did the same. They immediately started to strip out of the navy blue jumpers, which left them dressed in expensive business suits.

Once they made it through the alleyway and entered the parking lot that sat across the street, the robbers looked like lawyers and accountants stepping out of the stolen Dodge van, walking their separated ways, getting into separate vehicles, and exiting the parking lot.

Rico got into a black 2019 Range Rover with a waiting Tata. "Let's clear out, bae," he said, setting the saddlebag between his feet that held the MP-5.

Tata leaned over the console and stuck her tongue in her lover's mouth and kissed him with a hunger only a woman could have for a bad boy. Tata pulled away from Rico and looked into his eyes with lust, biting down on her bottom lip. She couldn't wait to get Rico home. Every time Rico pulled a robbery and made it back to her, it made her juices flow.

Tata pushed her Prada shades back on her face, put the Range in drive, and pulled out of the parking lot, singing along with Nicki Minaj. "I wanna be bad for you. I wanna be bad for you!"

***

"Shit, the Boone & Sons move was too sweet, slim," Rico said as he placed the last timepiece on the black marble table. The table was covered with various brands of jewelry and watches. The collection consisted of twelve Cartier watches, nine Presidential Rolex, ten Daytona Masters, seven Oyster Masters and four Yacht Masters with a string of diamond rings. Rico easily estimated he had $250,000 worth of jewelry on the table.

"That's real talk, Rico," Tone chimed in, picking up a platinum Oyster Master watch off the table and examining it with a lustful eye. "This beauty here is true perfection," Tone smiled and placed the watch on his wrist.

"Nigga, what the fuck you think you doing? I know you don't think you keeping that shit?" Rico questioned his partner.

"Damn, Rico, we never get a chance to keep none of this shit we take," Tone complained.

"I know, and that's how we stay out of them federal penitentiaries, too. You know the rules. We get rid of everything from the robberies."

Tone didn't want to argue with Rico, so he just took the watch off his wrist and laid it back down on the marble table.

Diesel just shook his head at Tone and fired the Backwood Cigar up. He really didn't like Tone too much. He knew Tone wanted to be something he truly wasn't, and that was a gangsta. Tone was a helluva stick-up artist under the leadership of Rico, but outside of that Tone was lost, and truth be told, that was one of the reasons Rico had brought Tone onto the crew.

Diesel let out a thick white cloud from his nose as he passed the burning Backwood to his role model.

"Before we hit the club tomorrow night, we going to meet back here and break the money down from the heist. That will give me enough time to meet Rau'f to trade the jewelry for cash," Rico stated in between pulls of the Backwood.

"That sounds like a plan to me, boss," Diesel said, rubbing his hands together. Nothing but two things got Diesel excited, and that was money and pussy. He was a sucka for both.

"Damn!" Diesel mumbled under his breath as Tata entered the room wearing a gray Chanel short set that was way too short, so short it was cutting into her booty all types of ways. Her sleeveless, form-fitted shirt stopped just below her round, melon-sized breasts. Tata's shirt showed off enough skin to let any admirer see the beautiful butterfly artwork that sat gracefully on her flat stomach like a painting on a canvas.

Diesel had another thing that got him excited, and that was Tata. His 20-year-old mind couldn't operate at its full capacity when she was in his presence.

"*Hola, papi*," Tata greeted Rico as she came into the room. Diesel loved how firm and thick Tata's legs were looking. All he could do was imagine them wrapped around him.

"*Mami*, what's good?" Rico stated, kissing Tata on her lips and continuing to talk to his men. "Tata and the girls will be casing our next caper. I think our next target will be Zales," Rico said, eyeing his partners and passing Tata the Backwood.

"When you going to let me and my girls pull our own heist, *papi*?" Tata asked, accepting the burning Backwood from her lover.

"Come on, *mami*, not now. Here we go with this shit again. I told you, when the time is right, we will put your team in the game. Until then, you keep casing our next potential target."

Tata sucked her teeth.

"Tsst! Damn, Rico, you always saying that, but you got us sitting on the sidelines watching all the action. Shit, a bitch get bored just watching," Tata said, hitting the Backwood.

"Yeah, but you bitches still get paid for sitting on the sideline, too."

"What, $5,000, Rico? That ain't no money, and you know it," Tata complained. "Phatmama and Zoey have been complaining about the pay you paying us for the work we be putting in. We feel like we should be getting a little more, casing the stores out and driving the getaway cars," Tata said, poking her luscious lips out.

"Well, until I see fit, that's what the fuck you bitches going to be getting paid for."

"*Papi,* you being petty as shit."

Tata's words were cut off mid-sentence by Rico's hand grabbing her throat. He squeezed tight. "Who the fuck you think your silly ass talking to?" Rico's face was inches away from Tata's, spit sprinkling on her face when he spoke.

"Come on, Rico. Chill, big homie," Diesel said, trying to verbally intervene.

"Nigga, stay the fuck outta mines," Rico shot back.

Tone just sat there with a grin on his face.

"What I tell you about trying to embarrass me in front of my niggas, T?" Rico spoke through clenched teeth.

Tata closed her eyes in submission. She knew trying to struggle or fight out of Rico's throat grip wouldn't do nothing but anger him and cause her further pain. "I'm sorry, Rico," Tata whispered.

Rico stared at Tata with anger, applying a little more

pressure to her throat before he let her go. Tata ran from the room with tears spilling out of her eyes.

Diesel admired how her ass bounced and jiggled as she ran from the room. He disliked how Rico could be so rough with someone so precious as Tata. Diesel looked at Rico. They briefly made eye contact, but neither of them made a comment about the situation that just took place.

"So, where were we?" Rico asked.

Tone filled in, "We going to meet up tomorrow night to get our take of the money, then we hitting the club."

"Yeah, that's right. So, if there isn't anything else to discuss, I got to go handle some shit," Rico said, nodding his head in the direction Tata fled.

They all dapped each other up, and Tone and Diesel left. Diesel just hoped Rico would take it easy on Tata for whatever plans he had for her.

Jibril Williams

Chapter 2

"Girl, that muthafucka put his hands on me," Tata cried into the phone to her second best friend, Phatmama.

"Tata, you lying!"

"Phatmama, I'm not lying! That fucker choke me right in front of Tone and Diesel."

"*Mami,* you know I'm dead serious when it comes to you. I'll bury his ass, Tata! Just give me the word, Tata. Fuck 'im," Phatmama said angrily through the other end of the phone.

"Naw, Phatmama, I can't let you do that, even though he been treating me shitty as fuck. I do love him, and I know he loves me when it comes down to it."

"Psh!" Phatmama couldn't believe her ears as to what her friend was saying.

Tata could hear her friend's frustration through her sigh, so she began to explain herself. "Without Rico, I wouldn't know where I would be right now. He reached out to me when my life seemed like it was a black ant on a black rock on a black night. Without him, I don't know how I would have made it through them last three years in the Feds."

"I know, Tata. Me, Zoey, and Jelli was right there with you. But that doesn't give him the fucking right to put his slimy-ass hands on you," Phatmama stated with an attitude. "He look out for all of us, and he even gave us a place to stay once we came home, but that shit still doesn't make it right. I'll kill his ass for hurting you."

"I know you would, Phatmama, but I still love him, though," Tata cried.

"What we need to do is hit our own lick and make some shit happen for ourselves," Phatmama said.

"And we will when the time is right," Tata sniffled.

Rico walked into the bedroom and stared at Tata with a

17

sympathetic look on his face.

"Phatmama, let me call you back?" Tata said, hitting the end button on her iPhone. She laid the phone next to her on the queen size bed and locked her eyes on the Angelia Davis photo that decorated the master bedroom wall.

Rico walk over to the foot of the bed. "I'm sorry, *mami*," he said, reaching out and touching one of Tata's pretty toes. He loved how her toes looked with the peach-colored nail polish on them.

Tata drew her feet back and tucked them under her in a fetal position.

"Tata, I'm sorry, baby. I didn't mean to choke you."

Tata was thinking to herself, *how in the hell someone don't mean to choke to you?*

"I lost my cool," Rico pleaded.

Tata ignored Rico. She knew despite the fact she loved him, she was in a bad relationship. Rico kept her where she was constantly depending on him. If she wanted to leave, she couldn't because she had no money or resources.

Rico crawled on the bed, straddled her, and began to kiss her tears. "Mwah. Mwah. I'm sorry, bae."

"Why you choke me in front of your friends, Rico?" Tata questioned with watery eyes.

Rico sighed. "You know how shit is, *mami*. I let you disrespect me in front of the same nigga's I dictate to, they would see that and lose respect for me, and I can't have that shit," Rico retorted, trying to justify his actions.

"That shit was uncalled for." Tata wiped tears and snot from her eyes and nose with the back of her hand.

"I know, *mami*, and I'm sorry." Rico kissed Tata on the cheek. He turned her face toward his and kissed her on the lips. She didn't resist. She let his tongue invade her mouth. She sucked on his tongue as if it was a fragile piece of candy.

The Heart of a Savage

Rico maneuver his body in between Tata's thighs and worked her Chanel shorts over her hips, exposing her neatly trimmed love garden. He threw her shorts to the floor. He could tell she was ready to accept his love stick by the moistness that covered her love rose. Tata always had the ability to stay wet under any condition. Rico was feverishly eager to plant his love stick deep into Tata's love garden.

Rico released his manhood from his Polo jeans. His pipe stood firm and straight. Taking the head of his manhood, Rico sliced open Tata's rose and plunged deep into her. Rico didn't stop until his balls were resting against his lover's sacred garden.

"Ooh, Rico, yes! Deep like I like it, *papi!*" Tata moaned, gripping Rico's ass cheeks, inviting him deeper into her.

Tata's insides squeeze tight around Rico's throbbing dick. Rico grinded hard into Tata, fulfilling her request to go deeper. Rico tossed Tata's firm, thick legs over his shoulder and, without delay, he quickly caught a strong, steady rhythm. *Smack, smack, smack!* Rico's nuts slapped against Tata's asshole.

"*Mami,* this pussy is so good. Whose pussy is this?" Rico stated, gliding in and out of Tata.

"Mm, *papi!* It's yours. Please go deeper and harder, *papi.* I'm cumming," Tata cried out. It was never hard for Tata to reach her climax while Rico served her in this position.

Tata's legs began to shake uncontrollably. All they could hear in the room were moans of pleasure and the sexual gushing sound of Rico's love sword stabbing in and out of Tata's woman cave.

"Oh, *papi,* here it comes. Ooh! Ooh! I'm cumming, *papi.*" Tata made an ugly fuck face and shook hard, releasing her honey dew all over Rico's dick.

Seeing Tata make her fuck face and seeing the thick

creaminess of her love box coat him took Rico to the edge. He just hated that he didn't get a chance to fuck Tata from the back before he could cum. Tata's back shots was something serious.

Rico's nuts drew up, and his manhood expanded to the max. He bit down on his bottom lip and gave Tata one last thrust before he pulled out and shot his load all over her stomach.

Tata looked at him like he had lost his damn mind. She stared at him as a glaze of sweat coated his face and he breathed hard.

Rico finally made eye contact with Tata. "What?" he said, looking at her strangely and removing her legs from his shoulders.

"When you start busting on me? That's some shit you do when you first start fucking with a bitch."

"Tata, I'm not trying to hear that shit. I just got caught up in the moment," he replied.

Tata searched his face for the lie, and she seen it. When Rico lied, he always narrowed his eyes and couldn't make eye contact with her, so seeing this made her dig farther. "Rico, do you have another bitch or a bitch knocked up somewhere?" Tata asked.

"Tata, miss me with that silly-ass shit you talking. We just had make-up sex, and now you started with the bullshit," Rico stated bitterly, crawling out of bed and placing his now-limp member back in his Polo jeans.

Tata paused and watched Rico for a minute. "So, it's not another bitch, and you don't have a bitch pregnant, so it must be you don't want to have kids with me. Because you always nut in me, and now you not."

"*Mami*, you blowing this shit out of proportion." Rico walked into the bathroom, coming back with a damp towel so Tata could clean his man juices off herself. "Listen, *mami,* there's no other bitch. There's no other bitch running around here carrying my seed. I just got caught up in the moment," Rico said with so much sincerity in his voice that Tata wanted to believe him. But the streets had taught her the eyes tell true lies, and Rico's eyes was telling a big, fat lie. But for now she would pay closer attention to her man.

"Here, baby, I got a little something for you." Rico handed Tata the most amazing toe ring she ever saw.

"Oh, shit, *papi!*" Tata's eyes lit up like the moon on a dark night. The diamonds in the ring looked like clear blue water, She counted the six stones in the platinum band. Tata placed the ring on her toe next to her big toe. She stuck her foot out to see how the ring looked on her toe. "Rico, I love it."

"I love it, too," Rico replied, eyeing Tata's still-exposed pussy. He licked his lips.

Tata caught on to the sexual undertone in Rico's voice and saw he was eye-fucking her cornbread muffin. She drew her knees back to her chest and said seductively in her native tongue, "*Tratame como una galleta de Oreo. Comeme de adentro pa fuera,*" which meant 'treat me like a Oreo cookie, eat me from the inside out.'

Rico smiled and obliged Tata's request.

***

"Oh my God, auntie, I'm feeling the hell outta this toe ring," Tata's 16-year-old niece said in awe as she stared down at the toe ring that decorated and highlighted Tata's foot.

"I like the ring, too, but your grown ass need to watch your damn mouth," Tata said, checking her niece Ski. "And where is your mother?"

Ski sucked her teeth. "She getting out the truck with her slowpoke butt. You know she is pregnant? She been throwing up all morning," Ski said with a little irritation in her voice. She hated the thought of her mother bringing a baby into the world. She was the only child, and she was spoiled rotten. Ski couldn't fathom the thought of her having to share her mother with some one else.

"Pregnant? Girl, get your ass in this house and stop spreading all your mother business. She haven't even told me she was pregnant yet, and here you go spilling the tea on your mother," Tata said, checking her fast-ass niece for the second time in five minutes.

Ski just rolled her eyes and walked past her aunt like she didn't hear a damn word she just said.

Tata stepped out on the porch to wave her sister in. Tina was sitting in her cocaine-white QX 60 Infinity truck, talking on her phone. Tina seen Tata and thrown up a finger, gesturing for Tata to give her a minute. Tata went back in the house to continue to get ready to head out to club Aqua. Tata knew Phatmama, Zoey, and Jelli would be there soon, so she headed straight to the bathroom for her quick shower.

Phatmama, Zoey, Jelli, and Tata all did a bid in the Feds at Hazleton F.C.I., West Virginia. Instantly the women became inseparable and a force to be reckoned with on the prison yard. Phatmama was doing a seven-year prison sentence for selling illegal firearms while she was enlisted in the Marine Corps. She received a dishonorable discharge for her deeds. Jelli's boyfriend at the time turned state's evidence on her and implemented her as a getaway driver in one of the nine bank robberies he committed, which led Jelli to do seven and a half years in Hazleton.

Zoey, however, did six years for manslaughter. Zoey was a golden glove champion at one time. She went to happy hour with a group of friends when a dude thought it was okay to grab a handful of her booty. Being under the influence and hot tempered was a bad combination for Zoey. She hit the dude with a solid jab that snapped his head back, but misjudged. When Zoey threw her knockout punch, it connected with the dude's windpipe, crushing it.

Tata, on the other hand, did a five-year bid for identity theft and fraud. Tata was the brains and had a special way of making people march to her drumbeat.

Tata used Dove body wash to lather her body. She loved how the silky body wash made her skin feel. She rubbed her soapy hands over her breasts, and on contact the Dove body wash made her nipples become hard. Her thoughts immediately turned to Rico. Tata rubbed her hand over her private area, and she still could feel the soreness from the pounding Rico put on her earlier. She bit down on her bottom lip, but shook her thoughts from her mind. Tata knew if she entertained her thoughts, she was going to be late, and she wasn't going to keep her girls waiting because she knew them bitches would fuck around and leave her. So she finished showering.

Twenty minutes later, after moisturizing her body down with cocoa butter lotion and winding her 28-inch Brazilian weave into a high ponytail, Tata stepped into a coffee-brown Michael Kors sleeveless dress that hugged her body with perfection. Tata was ready to show off and show out tonight. She double-checked her make-up, which didn't consist of much but MAC lip-gloss and a little mascara. Tata was naturally beautiful. She had somewhat of an exotic look to her. Being black and Puerto Rican done her body wonders. Standing a perfect 5'7", her 143-pound frame had more curves than a back road. Her B-cups was mounded high and there wasn't a sag or stretch mark in sight. Her thighs and hips were so impeccable and blessed with the most prefect curves that every man and woman had a desire to touch them, but what made muthafuckas want to stalk Tata was her 40-inch round, ghetto booty that shook like Jell-O no matter what she was doing. Tata favored

Juju off *Love & Hip Hop,* but the only thing that set them apart was Tata had a set of luscious and suck-able lips on her that any porn industry would have paid her a lot of money to wrap around a big ol' dick and make a movie out of it.

Tata slid her size six feet inside her cream-colored Red Bottoms, doused herself with Chanel No.5, and grabbed her cream-colored Michael Kors clutch purse off the bed and she was ready to go.

"Damn, bitch, about fucking time your ass came downstairs. We was finna leave that ass," Jelli said, jumping off the sofa and giving Tata a hug. "And, damn, you are rocking the fuck out that dress." Jelli admired Tata in her form-fitting dress. This was Tata's best friend. They were the tightest out of the four.

Phatmama stood to the side and examined Tata's face. Tata could tell she really wanted to address the issue of Rico putting his hands on her, but before Phatmama could do so, Zoey spoke.

"Y'all bitches ready? I'm ready to get my drink on and stunt on these hos."

"Hell yeah, *mami*! Let's go. I'm ready to party," Tina said, getting off the sofa and pulling her white-and-black pin-stripe Prada slacks out of the creases of her pussy. Tina's pants was so tight she left nothing to the imagination as to what her coochie would look like.

Even though Tina and Tata was blood sisters they looked nothing alike. That was due to them having different fathers. Tina was a creation of a Mexican and Puerto Rican, but she looked more Mexican than anything else. She was slim, a 5'9" dame who had a set of charming hazel-green eyes that could make any pimp submit his ho over to her. Now, Tina didn't have that mammoth-size backside Tata had, but she was strong in the chest department. Tina had the type of chest that, when a man met her, it was his goal to bed her and bust a fat, juicy nut on her chest just to say he did that.

All the women grabbed their purses and phones and headed to the door. "Oh, hold up. Aye, Ski!" Tata called out.

"Yeah, auntie," Ski responded, coming from the back of the house.

"Don't have no boys in my house with your fast-ass. You think you slick."

"Tsk!" Ski sucked her teeth and acted like she didn't even hear her aunt. Tata rolled her eyes at her niece and walked out the door.

The four beautiful babes jumped in Zoey's all-burgundy Audi truck. Zoey was always the designated driver when they went out because she did the least drinking out of the bunch. Give her one Long Island Ice Tea and she was good.

Zoey backed out of Tata's driveway and turned the volume up, letting Cardi B's "Bodak Yellow" pump from the SUV's speakers. The women immediately chimed in and begun to sing with Cardi B. "I don't dance, I make money moves. These are Red Bottoms, these are bloody shoes."

Phatmama sparked up the loud pack she had twisted tightly in a Backwood. She took a deep pull of the smoke and let the high quality weed work its magic. She passed it to Tata, which Tata gladly accepted.

"Damn, *mami,* this weed is the truth. I only took three pulls, and I can feel the effects of it already," Tata said in between pulls.

Zoey navigated the truck toward the highway. "Tata, stop talking and pass the blunt," Zoey said, playing.

Tata flapped her extended eyelashes and rolled her eyes. "Here, girl, with your geeking ass." Tata handed the good smoke to Zoey. She was a little upset she didn't fully get the buzz she wanted before she had to pass the Backwood.

Zoey wasn't paying Tata's attitude any mind. She grabbed

the Backwood from Tata and kept rapping along with Cardi B.

"Oh, shit, here you all go." Tata pulled out three manila envelopes and passed Zoey, Jelli, and Phatmama one each. "This the money for the job," Tata stated.

Phatmama promptly open her envelope and started counting her money. Zoey opened the glove department and stored her money there.

"Rico wants us casing the next target and start working out the details. He said that shit needs to be airtight," Tata stated, cracking her window to let some of the smoke seep out the truck.

"I ain't doing shit! Fuck that bitch-ass nigga. He going to put his hands on you, and now he want us to plan another job? Fuck him," Phatmama said with her face balled up.

"Hold on! Rico put his hands on you?" Tina asked Tata from the back seat.

"He didn't really hit me. He just somewhat choked me."

"Yeah, right in front of Tone and Diesel," Phatmama chimed in.

Jelli just shook her head in disbelief.

"Tata, all the shit Mommy went through in an abusive relationship when we was growing up, you going to allow Rico to do that to you?" Tina asked with sadness in her eyes.

Tata really didn't want to discuss the situation about Rico putting his hands on her. "I love Rico, and it was just one time," Tata tried to defend her lover, but knowing this wasn't his first time putting his hands on her.

"Yeah, Mommy said the same thing, but that didn't stop Paul from beating the fuck outta her," Tina retorted.

Tata's eyes instantly became misty. She remembered to vividly the day Paul killed her mother. She turned her head and looked out the window, trying to will herself not to cry.

"Don't you remember the promise our mother made us

make to her before she died?" Tina questioned Tata.

Tata remained silent. Tina lean up from the back seat and placed a hand on her sister's shoulder. Tata turned her head and faced her sister.

"We promised her if a man ever put his hands on us, we would kill his ass." The look in Tina's eyes was intense.

Tata nodded her head up and down in agreement. "If he does it again, I will fulfill the promise I made to Mommy," Tata said.

"No. *We* will fulfill our promise to Mommy," Tina said sternly, letting her sister know she had her back 100%.

Jibril Williams

Chapter 3

The conversation the women just had left an awkward silence in the truck. Tata desperately wanted to change the mood and get her friend's thoughts off her dysfunctional love life, so what better thing to do than put someone else in the hot seat and under the spotlight?

"Tina, when was you going to tell me I was going to be receiving another niece, or this time a little nephew?" Tata asked, turning around in the passenger seat to face her sister.

"What the? You pregnant?" Phatmama blurted out.

"Bitch, who did you let knock your ass up?" Jelli questioned, wanting Tina to spill all her tea.

"How the hell you know I was pregnant?" Tina said with a light attitude. She was slightly offended Tata would question her about being pregnant in front of her friends, and it didn't make the situation easier for her with Tata and her friends shooting all those question at her at 100 miles going north. Shit like this reminded Tina how ratchet Tata and her friends could be.

"Your little hot-in-the-ass daughter spilled the tea about you being pregnant. She told me about the morning sickness and all," Tata replied.

Tina made a mental note to have a serious talk with Ski about running her mouth about shit that don't concern her. "Yeah, I'm expecting a little one," Tina said, rubbing her flat stomach.

"When did this happen?" Tata curiously wanted to know, because she hadn't seen her sister booed up with someone in a hot D.C. minute.

"I'm going on nine weeks. I just went to the doctor's last week, just to confirm it."

"Who is the daddy?" Jelli asked for the second time.

Tina rolled her eyes at Jelli. Tina really didn't know what to tell her women about who the daddy was, but they was all ears. She couldn't tell the truth about the real identity of her baby daddy. If she did, all hell would break loose, so she did the next best thing in a moment like the one she was in. She lied her ass off.

"Well, you don't really know him. He was a little buddy I had that comes through from time to time when I was having them lonely nights."

"You got pregnant by a booty call nigga?" Jelli said with her face balled up, a hint of judgment in her voice.

Phatmama popped her lips at Jelli's line of questions. Zoey turned the radio down some so she could hear Tina's answer.

"It's not even like that. And bitch, don't judge me." Tina gave Jelli that don't-fuck-with-me look.

"So, when I'm going to meet this guy? And how he feels about you having a baby?" Tata asked.

Tina took a deep breath. "I haven't told him about the baby yet."

"Why not?" Tata said with a concerned look on her face.

"Because he's over in D.C. jail fighting a gun charge, and I didn't want to add any more stress than I have to on him." Tina turned her head and looked out the window.

"Damn!" Zoey let the word slip out as she stopped the truck at a red light. The thought of another child growing up without their father didn't sit right with Zoey, even if it was for a few months, a few week, or a few years. Children needed their dads.

"Hey, pick that head up, *mami*! He might not be there for you right now, but I'm here for you, and we are here for you. We gotcha, *mami*," Tata stated, reaching into the back seat and turning Tina's head her way to gaze into her eyes.

"Thanks, sis."

"You are not in this alone," Phatmama chimed in.

Tina was thankful for the gestures her sister and friends showed her, but only if they really knew who was the child's father was, they would be having a whole different type of conversation.

"Who is the father? And do you need help telling him you are pregnant?" Tata asked.

Tina hesitated. "Um, you remember Cam from around Berry Farms?"

"What! Tina, you let that young nigga get you pregnant?" Tata blurted out in shock. Jelli shook her head in disbelief.

"I know I really fucked up, but shit just happened. I didn't mean to give the boi some pussy. Shit just happened. And no, I don't need help telling him. I will do that next week when I go to visit him. Now, can we please get out my business and back into the clubbing mood?" Tina stated, pulling a small mirror out of her clutch and examining her make up.

Tata dropped the interrogation. She could only imagine how embarrassed Tina was by getting pregnant by Cam's young ass. Tata had only met Cam twice, and from his low-maintenance appearance, he wasn't Tina's type. Tina claimed he was a great conversationalist, so that was why she was entertaining him. But Tata knew opposites attract like magnets, so a person could never really say who they would fuck or fall in love with.

Tata was happy she was going to be having another niece or nephew, and even happier she was no longer the center of her girls' attention. She turned the music back up and got back to grooving with Cardi B.

***

Thirty minutes later, arriving at club Aqua on Connecticut Avenue, the ladies had a good buzz going from the loud pack Phatmama blessed them with. When they stepped out of the truck, they checked their makeup and applied extra lip-gloss to their lips.

They made their way to the front of the club where people had been waiting a good 45 minutes to get in the club. They received some evil stares from some of the ladies standing in line, but Tata and her clique didn't care. They didn't pay the unfortunate and unimportant any attention as they strutted past them and flung their Brazilian weaves over their shoulders and pranced hard to the club entrance.

Jelli had the men in line going into overdrive. All the men she passed unintentionally grabbed their crotches. Jelli's name spoke volumes. No matter what she wore – shorts, skirt, jeans, or leggings – her 42-inch ass couldn't be contained, and tonight was no different. The gray Michael Kors slacks she squeezed into with no panties on had her ass shaking and bouncing harder than a stripper twerking for a $100 tip at Stadium strip club. The white, strapless, silk Michael Kors shirt was form fitting, but her breasts in it shook and bounced just as hard as her booty did. Jelli was a straight cutie with her loving bubble eyes and her Colgate smile. She was the humblest out of the group. Jelli stood a good 5'6", weighing in at 152 pounds. She kinda favored Taraji P. Henson, but she was just a whole lot thicker.

They made it to the entrance and the bouncer let them in with no problem. Rico had made this happen. Him frequently visiting the club and being a big spender at the establishment gave him special privileges that trickled down to Tata and her girls.

The floor-to-ceiling windows were tinted where no one could see in the club, but they could see out. The bright red carpet stretched across the floor enhanced the two-level club's liveliness.

It seemed like everyone came out to party tonight, for some reason or another. The black crystal chandelier hanging from the ceiling marked club Aqua as the place to be.

The women headed straight to the bar, turning heads in the process. "Give us a bottle of Ace of Spades apiece," Tata told the light-skinned, freckle-faced barmaid, handing her a few crisp bills. The big-face money looked funny under the club lights.

The barmaid popped the champagne for the ladies and went on to her next customer who was flagging her down at the other end of the bar.

"Let's make a toast, bitches!" Tata yelled over the music.

Jeremiah and Ty Dolla's song "Paris" was banging through the club speakers. Tina and Phatmama's bodies was swaying to the beat. Tina had her eyes closed, thinking about her new, forbidden baby daddy of her unborn child.

All four women held their bottles in the air. "To some of the realist and sexiest bitches that this city done seen." Everyone took an obese gulp of champagne. Everyone except for Tina. She just clutched her bottle in her hand, giving whatever onlookers she may have had the impression she was part of the circle of drinkers.

The ladies proceeded to make their way to the V.I.P. section where they knew Rico and his crew would be. The D.J. changed the song, and Jelli and Tata strutted and danced to the beat of Cardi B's song "Drip." A few partygoers tried to flag Tata down, but she ignored all call-outs, leaving a group of men lusting on her backside.

"Shit, it's packed in here tonight," Phatmama yelled over the music as they climbed the stairs to the second level of the club where the V.I.P. section was located.

"And the night is still young, so you know this going to get shoulder-to-shoulder in here before the night is over. I'm so glad we got V.I.P. so I don't have to worry about some bum-ass niggas trying to squeeze on my ass all night," Jelli said with a fake frown on her face.

"Bitch, who you think you fooling? You know damn well you like the attention that juicy ass brings you," Tina said, pinching Jelli on her booty.

"Tina, you just jealous you don't have a ass like mines," Jelli shot back at her.

"Girl, whatever. You would love to believe I was jealous."

"So why every chance you get you poking and squeezing on my ass?" Jelli questioned.

"Because I admire your booty, but I'm never jealous," Tina stated, sticking her tongue out at Jelli and giving her a smile. The women shared another hearty laugh.

"You two are straight craz–"

Tata's sentence was cut short. What she saw made her words get lost in her throat. Walking into V.I.P., Rico was being entertained by a half-naked beauty who was dancing in his lap, grinding hard on his dick that stood hard and fighting to bust out of his Tom Ford slacks. Tata's heart began to beat rapidly, and it seemed like all the blood in her body rushed to her head and caused her to see red. What really sent Tata's anger into overtime was the Pinky look-alike chick had her top down on her dress and had Rico's face buried deep between her silicon breast. Rico had the woman's dress up in the back and had her butta-soft ass in the palms of his hands.

Tata charge the woman, grabbing her by the hair, and snatched her out of Rico's lap. The woman's hair was snatched with so much force it made a popping sound. "Argh!" the woman yapped out in pain. Tata slung her to the floor.

Jelli went into straight football mode and treated the woman's head like a football, giving it a punt like she was kicking for an NFL team. The woman let out another cry and covered her face up as blood began to leak from her face.

"Rico! What the fuck you think you doing, *papi*?" Tata said, picking up a drink off the table and throwing it in Rico's face.

The Hennessey splashing Rico's face knocked the smirk he wore off of it. The dark brown liquid dripped down and stained his Tom Ford shirt and pants.

Rico look at his spoiled clothes and at the onlookers in the V.I.P. section. Rage leapt into him, and with one quick motion and the striking precision of a king cobra, he sprung from the lounge couch, striking Tata with an open hand. *Whap*! And before she could react or feel the pain from the slap, Tata was greeted with a backhand. *Whap*! This knocked her down on top of the woman who, moments ago, she'd given a whiplashing to.

Rico raise his black gator in the air to bring it down on Tata's head. Phatmama advanced with the quickness of a mongoose. She placed the blade of her alloy knife to Rico's neck. Its sharp teeth bit into his flesh.

"Bitch-ass nigga, if you do, I will kill you right where you stand," Phatmama stated though clenched teeth, applying pressure to the knife on Rico's throat.

Rico's foot hung in midair. He was afraid to move an inch. Phatmama had a look in her eyes Rico had never encountered from her before. Her look told Rico she was very well capable of carrying out her threats if he brought his foot down on Tata.

Rico's eyes met Tone's. Tone's hand eased to his waist. Rico mouthed the word "No," giving the order for Tone to stand down.

Zoey held Tina at bay.

"Come on, Phatmama, put the knife away before you do something you'll regret," Rico said, barely moving his lips.

"I'll do that once your dog-ass put your foot down where it belongs."

Rico came into compliance. The V.I.P. stood frozen. Tina stood there with fire in her eyes, looking at Rico with her face balled up into a knot. Rico placed his gator back on the V.I.P.

carpet.

Tata jumped up and bolted from the room, holding her face with tears spilling between her fingers.

Phatmama slowly removed the blade from Rico's neck and whispered, "The next time, you will fall victim to the axe."

Rico didn't know what the hell Phatmama was talking about, but he was glad she removed her knife from his neck."

Chapter 4

Tata bumped into people as she zigzagged through the crowed club with tears still running down her face. The people in the club looked at her as if she was crazy as she damn near knocked over a drunken woman who was way too drunk to complain about Tata bumping into her. Tata's face was displaying what her heart was feeling, and that feeling was pain. She couldn't believe Rico showed his ass the way he did in front of her friends. *How did I allow myself to get in this situation?* Tata thought to herself.

Exiting the club, the night air hit her, bringing coolness to her skin. She didn't know where she was going, she just knew she needed to get away from club Aqua and the big hand of Rico.

Tata seen Diesel's smoke-gray Range pull up in the parking lot. Tata ran to the Rover at full speed, snatching the passenger side door open and jumping in unannounced.

"What the fuck?" Diesel said, reaching for the Glock 40 that rested on his lap. Tata caught him off guard, and he wasn't feeling that. "Tata, what's your muthafuckin' problem, hopping in my shit like you fucking crazy? I almost shot your ass!"

"Please, Diesel, just take me home," Tata begged.

Diesel, seeing Tata with water flooding her eyes and a slight swollen face, lowered his aggression and let concern take its place. "Are you alright? You been fighting?" He reached over and tried to turn Tata's face toward him so he could inspect her damages.

Tata yanked her head from his grasp. "Please, Diesel, just take me home. All I want to do is go home," Tata whispered as she leaned her head back on the soft leather headrest.

Diesel knew if Rico wasn't out here with Tata taking her home, then he was the cause of Tata's bruised face and distress.

Diesel let out a long sigh and shook his head, easing the luxury truck into gear and navigated the truck out of the parking lot.

He pushed the Range Rover at an easy 55 miles-per-hour as the sounds of Anthony Hamilton's song "Float" flowed through the speakers. Diesel couldn't help but glance at Tata's chocolate limbs. The streetlights glowed off her cocoa butter-coated legs. His eyes roamed up her thighs. The short dress she wore left a lot to admire. He discreetly licked his lips and placed his wandering eyes back on the road, adjusting his dick in his pants.

"Why you let Rico hurt you the way he does?" Diesel asked without looking at Tata.

With her eyes closed, she responded, "Why do you give a fuck?"

"I care because you are way too fine to be running around with a swollen face and ruined mascara."

"You think you can do better?" Tata questioned Diesel while still keeping her eyes closed.

"Fuck yeah! And you won't have to worry about me doing some geeking-ass shit to you like putting my hands on you."

The words Diesel just spoke ran to Tata's heart. Diesel knew nothing of what transpired tonight, but without saying, he knew she had fallen victim to being Rico's punching bag. Tears forced their way from under Tata's closed eyelids.

Diesel noticed the glistening of Tata's tears when he glanced over at the woman he so badly lusted for. He eased his foot off the gas and wiped some of Tata's tears away. She didn't resist his touch this time. She welcomed his touch. At this point she needed some affection. Tata placed her hand on his and kissed his knuckles. The softness of Tata's lips aroused Diesel faster than lightening.

Diesel pulled up to Tata's Laurel, MD home. He reached over, taking a finger and turning Tata's head toward him. He slowly kissed her. He was hesitant at first until Tata welcomed him by greeting his tongue with hers. Diesel sucked hard on her bottom lip, savoring every drop of Tata's juicy lips.

Diesel's hands shot down between Tata's thighs. The liner of her panties was hot and moist. He pushed her Victoria's Secret panties to the side. He thumbed her pearl and inserted two fingers deep into her secret garden. Tata's love cave was so wet it made gushing sounds as Diesel worked his fingers in and out of her.

Diesel brought his hand from between Tata's legs. He examined the sticky substance Tata's honey pot produced. Her pussy juices were thick as honey. Diesel placed his fingers in his mouth and sucked them clean. "Mm! You taste delicious."

For the first time, Tata opened her eyes. Diesel unbuckled his Gucci belt and released his member from his Gucci pants. He grabbed Tata's hand and placed it on his manhood. Tata grabbed it and squeezed it, feeling its thickness. Diesel's dick thumped in her hand like it had a pulse of its own.

Diesel went in for another kiss. He stuck his tongue deep and hungrily into Tata mouth.

Tata worked her hand up and down Diesel's shaft. Her body was telling her yes, but her heart was screaming no. An illustration of Rico invaded her mind like a thief in the night, which confirmed what her heart was saying.

"I'm sorry, Diesel. We can't do this," Tata said, pulling her lips away from Diesel and releasing his member from her hand. Tata pulled her dress back down.

"Come on, Tata, let me take your pain away." Diesel went to grab Tata, which she rejected by turning her face. Diesel paused and stared at Tata for a moment. He put his now-deflating penis back into his pants. "I can understand that you need some time, and when you are ready, I'll be here, waiting and willing to protect you," Diesel stated with such profoundness that Tata instantly wanted to believe him.

"Thank you, Diesel. That means a lot to me, but I got to handle shit with Rico. I'm really not this easy type of woman I'm displaying tonight. I'm just an emotional wreck right now…. Who the fuck is that?" Tata said, looking past Diesel to the woman who was sitting on the steps that led to her house.

Tata climbed out of the Range, straightened out her dress, and made her way up the walk leading to her house. As she got closer, she could see a woman holding a child that looked to be about a year old. "Excuse me, can I help you? Why are you sitting in front of my house, *mami*?" Tata asked as she approached the woman.

The woman stood up and slightly bounced the sleeping baby in her arms. The woman looked familiar. "Yeah, I'm looking for Rico, my daughter's father," the woman stated with a little attitude, giving Tata the impression the woman knew who she was.

Tata caught a side glimpse of the child, and even from that angle she couldn't deny the resemblance the child and Rico had. This revaluation was like a blow to Tata's stomach, but Tata still didn't want to come to grips with the truth that stood before her. "Bitch, what you mean your daughter's father? Rico don't have no fucking kids," Tata said with her nose flaring.

"Listen, Tata. I have my daughter with me. I'm not looking for any trouble out of you. My beef is with Rico."

"Bitch, how the fuck you know my name? What, you and Rico punk-ass been pillow-talking about me?"

Shit hit Tata like a .45 in the chest. The woman who stood in front of her was the same woman who ran up on Rico's car a few months ago when she and Rico was pulling out of the gas station. Rico didn't stop the car. He kept going and claimed he didn't know the woman.

"It's not a secret that me and Rico done had a conversation or two about you. He was talking about leaving you, then a few months ago he just stop coming around and calling. I even heard he had another bitch pregnant, but I'm to the point I just want Rico to step up and take care of his daughter."

It was obvious Rico had dealt Tata the ultimate dish of betrayal by having a baby on her with another woman. Tata knew it wasn't her or the woman's fault.

"What's you name, *mami*?" Tata asked.

"CeeCee."

"And the baby?"

"Nikky."

"CeeCee, from now on, I'm the child's father." Tata reached into her purse, pulled out a stack of hundreds, and handed them to CeeCee.

CeeCee wanted to question her about her statement, but Tata possessed a look in her eyes that told her not to. She was just thankful she had some money now to pay rent and feed her baby. "Thank you," CeeCee mumbled. She gave Tata her number, then went and got in a late-model Lexus and drove away.

Tata's tears spilled again for the hurt Rico has caused her. She intended to fill her promise to her deceased mother.

"Aye, Tata, you cool?" Diesel yelled from his truck still parked in front of her house.

Tata spun on her heels, wiping tears from her face. She walked toward Diesel's truck using her diva walk. She walked around the truck to the passenger side while holding eye contact with Diesel. Sliding inside, Tata laid her hand on Diesel's crotch and seductively whispered. "Diesel, I'm ready. Please fuck me."

***

Phatmama called Tata for the fifth time that night since the incident transpired at the club with Rico. The thought of Rico slapping Tata to the floor like a common ho didn't sit well with her.

"Are you going to play on your phone all night, or you going to come play with this dick?" Bless asked, lying on his king size bed naked, stroking his 11-inch dick in an up-and-down motion.

He and Phatmama met a few weeks ago at the Donovan House, an upscale establishment. He'd been blowing Phatmama's phone up ever since they exchanged numbers, so when he spotted her at the club last night and got her attention, she was down to blow some frustration on him that was intended for Rico.

Phatmama stood at the foot of the bed in her birthday suit, exposing her brown nipples that stood firm on her double-C breasts. Phatmama was slightly on the chubby side, but she was shapely and had a nice, round booty to compliment her chubbiness. Her caramel skin tone made her look as if she had basked in the sun daily. The dim room light glowed off her skin.

Phatmama crawl onto the bed seductively, making eye contact with Bless. She couldn't believe Bless had made such an amateur mistake by bringing her to a place where he lay his head. This nigga was moving like a lame. He even bragged about how much money he was getting in the streets and showed her a duffle bag full of money and drugs.

"I don't play with dicks. I work them," Phatmama said, taking control of Bless' manhood and slowly beginning to stroke him. Her small hands felt so soft against Bless' skin.

"Oh yeah, Phatmother!" Bless moaned.

Phatmama rolled her eyes at hearing Bless call her by the wrong name. "That's what you like?" Phatmama asked, planting a wet, juicy kiss on his dick head, making his love muscle twitch in her hand.

Bless lay there, enjoying the sensation Phatmama was giving him. He couldn't wait to beat Phatmama's guts in. He wanted to get the party started with some head. He placed his hand on the back of Phatmama's head, trying to guide her mouth down on his dick. "Come on, Phatmother, eat this dick. Stop playing wit' it."

Phatmama shook her head free from Bless' hand. "Bless, I don't need help finding or sucking your dick. Move your hand and lay back and let me bless you with this supa head," Phatmama retorted, kissing the head of Bless' dick again softly.

"Shit, that feel good. Ok, do ya thang," Bless stated, getting comfortable and laying his head back on his Burberry pillows.

Phatmama slowly and skillfully worked Bless in her mouth, inch after inch. The further she placed him in her mouth, the more his toes curled and cracked. "Hmm," Phatmama hummed on his dick while making all kinds of nasty slurping sounds with the saliva that oozed down onto Bless' nuts.

"Damn!" Bless yelled out at how supreme Phatmama's throat game was. Bless looked down at Phatmama. She was staring at him with a yard of dick in her mouth. Bless' dick stiffened. He knew if he kept watching his dick disappear in and out of Phatmama's mouth with the perfection of a porn star, he was going to explode. Bless laid back on the pillows again and closed his eyes.

Phatmama pulled the meat bat out of her mouth, letting off a popping sound. She took Bless' baby arm-sized dick and smacked it against her cheek, bringing his dick to even more stiffness. She placed him back in her mouth and wetted him back down in her saliva. Bless' toes cracked louder.

All of a sudden, the pleasure Bless was receiving was replaced by pain. Bless' eyes popped open, feeling something slice him under his dick head. Phatmama spit his dick head onto his stomach. She gripped a razor between her teeth.

"Argh! Fuck!" Bless screamed as blood erupted out of his headless dick like lava shot out of a volcano. Blood splattered his chest and sprayed Phatmama in the face.

She had The Last Exorcism look smeared across her face. Before Bless could fully react to his attacker, Phatmama spit the blade into her hand and, in one swift motion, she raked the razorblade across his stomach.

Bless jumped from the bed, holding his now-limp penis. Blood dripped from between his fingers. Standing up fully, Bless' insides spilled from his body. His intestines hung from his stomach and rested on the floor.

The whole scene was too much for Bless. His legs became weak, and his knees buckled.

Phatmama eased off the bed and made her way over to her Gucci purse, removing the razor-sharp combat knife. The same knife she held to Rico's throat earlier that night. The light reflected off the vicious-looking weapon.

Bless fought hard to put his insides back in. He was in extreme pain.

Phatmama admired her work. Her nipples hardened up like rock candy, and a tingle began to formulate between her legs.

"C-Come on, Phatmother, please!" Bless pleaded for his life.

Phatmama smirked while still maintaining that exorcism look. She raised the blade up over her head and brought it down into Bless' cranium, then gave the knife a twist.

Bless' body shook shortly.

Phatmama yanked the knife out of his head, letting his body fall completely to the floor. Bless lay there with his eyes still open. His brown eyes moments ago contained life. Now they were dull and showed no existence of life in them.

Phatmama went and grabbed the remote from the nightstand, selected Ella Mai's song "Tripping," and turned the volume up on the Bose system. She hit the shower and cleaned herself up. Twenty minutes later, she was dressed and ready to leave.

She bent down over Bless' body and hacked off his dick. She then went to the kitchen, found the microwave, tossed the dick in it, and set the timer for 20 minutes.

Phatmama went to retrieve the bag of money and drugs Bless showed her earlier. She left Bless' house with Ella Mai's song stuck in her head, so she started singing the catchy hook. "Trip-Trip-tripping on you."

Jibril Williams

Chapter 5

Tata lay in her bed, reflecting on the events that took place last night. She promised herself she wasn't going to shed another tear for Rico's lying dog-ass. She knew she was a good woman, but didn't understand why she was attracted to all the wrong types of niggas, the ones who truly don't know her worth because they never had a woman of her caliber. Now she understood why Rico wasn't cumming in her all of sudden when they had sex. His ass done went out and got another bitch pregnant.

"Fuck you, Rico!" Tata mumbled under her breath, getting even madder that Rico didn't come home last night, nor did he give her a call to apologize for his actions. But it wouldn't have made a difference since she met his baby mother CeeCee and their daughter Nikky.

Tata's eyes misted over. She was fighting the urge to cry.

She hopped outta bed and planted her ten pretty toes in the white carpet. She stood and stretched, pulling her lace panties out of her ass. Tata headed to the shower. She turned the water to her liking, stripped out of her panties and bra, and got under the showerhead. The hot water beat against her skin. She grab the loofa and Dove body wash. Tata scrubbed her body and let the Dove body wash clean her body and clear her mind.

She needed to formulate a plan to get away from Rico. Tata knew she had to step up and take charge of her life and be the boss bitch she knew how to be, but first things first, she needed to call a meeting with her clique ASAP.

Tata rinsed her body free of the body wash and stepped free from the shower. Brushing her teeth and oiling her body down, Tata stepped into a pair of Black Billionaire sweatpants. She threw on a white wife beater with no bra, letting the soft cotton brush against her nipples, bringing them to erection. She placed her hair in a high ponytail and stepped into a pair of white Prada flip-flops.

Grabbing her phone off the vanity, she seen she had over fifty missed calls and texts from her girls. What was odd was Tina hadn't called, not once.

She sent a group text telling her girls to meet her at IHOP in thirty minutes for brunch. She informed them this was a must-show meeting.

Tata dropped her smart phone into her Prada purse and slid some dark Prada shades over her eyes. She was ready to go.

Pulling up at the IHOP, Tata noticed Zoey's burgundy Audi truck. Parking her truck, Tata got out. Checking her surroundings, she didn't see Jelli's car or Phatmama's.

She made her way inside IHOP. The aroma from the food attacked her nose and activated the growls in her stomach. *Damn, I'm hungry*, Tata thought to herself, placing a hand over her stomach.

She saw Zoey and Jelli sitting in a corner booth. She walked over and removed her shades. "Where's Phatmama?" Tata questioned, taking a seat in the booth without looking at her friends.

"She hasn't got here yet. Me and Jelli rode together. She crashed at my place last night," Zoey stated.

Jelli searched Tata's face. She could sense a different Tata was seated across from her. "*Mami,* are you ok?" Jelli asked.

Tata looked at Jelli and Zoey for the first time. "I'm good, and shit is going to get better once our plan starts to manifest itself," Tata retorted firmly.

"I'm sorry I'm late," Phatmama said, sliding next to Tata in the booth and kissing her on the cheek.

"Are you ladies ready to place your orders?" the waitress asked, showing the group her pearly whites.

"Um, we going to do the buffet, but can you bring us a pitcher of orange juice and apple juice, please?" Tata ordered for them all.

"Okay, would that be all?" the waitress asked.

"Yes," Tata gave up a light-hearted smile.

"Before we get started, Tata, I don't appreciate you not retuning my calls last night after that shit went down at the club," Phatmama stated.

"No bullshit, slim, that was some wild shit," Jelli and Zoey chimed in, giving Tata the evil eye.

"I'm sorry about that, but some more crazy shit fell in my lap that needed my attention."

"Like what?" Zoey asked, getting all in Tata's business.

Tata let out a deep sigh and rubbed her temples. Her three comrades waited patiently for Tata to speak. "Don't you know this bitch-ass nigga got a whole fucking kid?"

"What? Who we talking about?" Jelli asked, looking confused.

"Rico!"

Phatmama and Zoey's mouths fell open in disbelief. Phatmama's heart rate went up a notch.

"I came home last night to find his babymoms on our doorstep with his daughter and all," Tata explained.

"Get the fuck outta here!" Zoey let the words spill out of her mouth unconsciously.

Jelli listened with a dissatisfied look on her face. "This nigga Rico is a wild, vicious dog, and he needs to be put down like one, too. He have the fucking nerve to put his hands on my girl, then his trifling ass have a whole baby on her?" Jelli said, pissed the fuck off and feeling bad for Tata.

Phatmama clenched her hands into tiny fists under the booth table.

"I know you whipped her ass, Tata?" Zoey asked, leaning

forward and placing her elbows on the table.

"Naw, I gave her my number and told her don't worry about Rico, I'll help her take care of the baby."

Zoey balled her face up. "Tata, you geekin' like shit. What part of the game is that bitch?"

"Listen, I'm not fighting bitches over Rico ho-ass. The bitch got played just like I got played, so my beef isn't with her. It's with Rico. And on top of that, her daughter didn't ask to be placed in this situation, or to be the daughter of a shit-eater like Rico. So there's no need to bring havoc to her or the child."

Jelli nodded her head up and down at Tata's reasoning.

"Here you go!" the waitress said, interrupting the ladies as she sat down the pitchers of apple and orange juice in the center of the table.

"Thank you!" Phatmama said, and all four women watched the waitress move to the next table before they started talking again.

"I called you bitches for a reason, and it's not to discuss Rico," Tata stated, breaking the silence, looking at her girls and making eye contact with each and every one of them.

"Speak on it, bitch," Jelli said.

"From this day forth, we making our own moves. We moving and conducting business like true boss bitches. It's time to get them hair salons and put our dreams of owning our club in motion. I have a plan, and I need you to trust me," Tata said.

The clique looked at Tata with sincerity in their eyes. "You know damn well we trust you," Zoey spoke for the group.

"Good, because we hitting Zales Jewelry," Tata stated in a whisper, pouring herself a glass of orange juice.

Phatmama smile hard.

"It's about fucking time. Let's get this paper." She viciously rubbed her hands together like she was trying to keep them warm.

"Do you think we're ready for that? And what about Rico and them?" Jelli questioned.

"Fuck Rico, and we are very capable of pulling the heist off," Tata said, taking a sip of orange juice.

"Count me in!" Zoey said, grabbing her a glass and helping herself to some apple juice.

Jelli looked at her girls and knew they was going to do it if she was in it or not. "Fuck it! Count me in."

"Alright, here is the plan. We going to case the job out just like we would do for Rico. We going to feed Rico the info on the heist, but we going to hit the Zales before Rico is scheduled to hit it."

"Ooh! You's a sneaky bitch. We got to watch you," Zoey said in her Cardi B voice. The table broke out in laughter.

"Girl, shut up and let's attack this buffet so I can share with you what I got in mind," Tata said, giggling.

"Ok, boss!" Jelli said with a wink of the eye and got up to go fill her plate with blueberry pancakes, eggs, bacon and French toast sticks. The rest of the girls followed suit.

***

Rico bit down on his bottom lip, enjoying the sloppy top he was receiving. "Damn, bae, make it touch the back of your throat again. That shit was boss."

His lover obliged his request and pushed him deep in her mouth until his mushroom head found its home at the back of her throat. She held him there and swirled her head in a small, circular motion while applying some pressure.

"Oh, shit, bae!" Rico moaned out loud, arching his back off the bed.

The woman brought Rico out of her mouth, making a slurping sound, jacked his dick up and down a few times, and pushed him back into her wet mouth.

Rico closed his eyes. He was in la-la land. He felt himself coming to a climax. He grab his baby mama's head and pumped feverishly into her mouth, making her gag with thick spit shooting from the sides of her mouth as it held Rico's dick. But she didn't dare come off his dick. She held her ground better than a veteran prostitute.

Since Rico had control of her head, she braced herself on her hands. She balled the sheets into her fist and closed her eyes. She work her head with the rhythm of Rico's thrusts.

Rico erupted in her mouth like a mad man as hot cum shot from his dick like a super soaker, coating her tonsils and throat. Rico's mistress was going for broke. She worked her jaw muscle and neck to drain every drop from him.

Rico laid back on the bed, trying to catch his breath while his Mexican beauty kissed and licked on his nuts. "I wish I could stay here with you forever," Rico said, wiping the sweat from his forehead.

"You can, *papi*," the woman said, releasing Rico's now slightly erected manhood. "All you got to do is leave her."

Rico look into the eyes of his lover and saw sincerity and desperation in them. "I'm going to, *mami*, but shit is complicated right now," Rico stated, reaching over and grabbing the half-smoked blunt, putting some heat to it, and taking a deep pull.

"I know the situation is complicated. I'm the one that's pregnant. But it's best to leave her now than wait until the baby gets here."

Rico rubbed the side of his lover's face with the tip of his fingers. Her beauty was always captivating to him. That was one of the reasons he was caught in this situation in the first place. "I know, baby. It's going to happen soon," Rico said, getting up from the bed.

"When, Rico? When is all this going to happen? I been waiting for a year now. If you not planning on leaving Tata, I'm going to abort the pregnancy."

Rico pounced and grabbed the pleading woman by the face. "Bitch, I'll beat—"

"Beat my ass like you did Tata's ass last night? If you think I'm going to let you beat on me, then you got me fucked up, Rico. I'll body your ass before I let that happen. Now, get your fucking hands off me."

Rico stared into the eyes of his lover and knew this one right here was different from Tata. He shook his head. "Please don't kill my seed. I'm going to leave Tata's ratchet-ass."

***

Diesel smoked on some high-grade kush. He had his hand inside his gym shorts, fumbling with his dick while he watched the highlights on ESPN. Every once in a while he would pull his hand out of his shorts and sniff his fingers, catching a light scent of Tata's sex from last night. The thought of the bottom of Tata's feet pressed against the dashboard of his truck as he pounded into her guts brought his dick to a slight erection. *Damn, I got to fuck her again*, he thought to himself. He knew he was wrong for fucking with Rico's woman, but it wasn't his fault Rico didn't know how to treat his queen. That was how he rationalized it in his young mind. Plus, he felt like someone was going to get the pussy anyway, so why not him?

Diesel picked his phone up off the couch. He couldn't get Tata out of his mind. Her soft skin was chilling, the way her lips felt wrapped around him. He sent her a good morning text with an emoji smiling face.

Instantly his phone vibrated. He saw it was Tata.

GM, mister, Tata replied, hitting him with the same smiling emoji.

Last night was the best, can't stop thinking about you, see look, Diesel typed and sent a dick pic with his text.

OMG!!! U so thick, can't stop thinking about last night either. I'm sitting here soaking wet. I would show you but I'm having brunch with my girls. Let's hook up later, Tata replied.

Diesel smiled hard and typed his response. *Okay slim, just hit me when you free.*

Ok Daddi, Tata texted back.

Diesel tossed his phone on the couch beside him and smiled. "She calling me 'daddy' already," Diesel said to himself, blowing clouds of smoke in the air.

Chapter 6

30 days later

"Give me the rundown, Jelli," Rico stated, lighting a cigarette and leaning against the wall.

"At approximately 9:15 a.m. the crew will enter Zales. Y'all will have a five-minute window. The store will be occupied with three employees: two clerks and one store manager. The store holds four display cases. One contains watches from Cartier, Rolex, Oyster Master to 41mm, Yacht Masters. Another display case holds their necklace and bracelet collection, and the other two cases hold the store's ring collection."

As Jelli was rattling off what the Zales heist contained in goods, Rico's mind was calculating the wealth of the heist.

"Behind the main display case there's a diamond cart that holds top-of-the-line diamonds and watches."

Tone listened intently. Diesel couldn't focus. He kept cutting his eyes at Tata, admiring her chocolate, shapely legs that threatened to burst the seams of her Gucci shorts that her legs spilled out of.

"Okay, Zoey, what you got?" Rico asked.

Zoey had compiled her info on her smart phone. "The store holds three cameras. One as you come into the store. You have one that rotates and hangs in the center of the store ceiling, and one right over top of the cash register. According to store security paperwork, there is also a silent alarm trigger behind the counter. So, when you go in there, you have to be on all them clerks and make sure that silent alarm doesn't get hit," Zoey said, seriously reading everything off her phone.

"Did you hear that, Diesel?" Rico said, catching him eyeing Tata for the third time today.

"Yeah, boss, I heard her," Diesel retorted, making eye

contact with Rico.

"Tomorrow we going to breeze through and check shit out at 9:30 a.m. to get a vibe check. This should be a walk in the park. We have hit much bigger stores," Rico stated, walking over to the table, pouring himself a shot of Hennessey, and downing it. "What's good with the hardware?" Rico asked Phatmama.

"Two .45s and a MP-5, clean, loaded, and ready to rock."

"Good. How is the escape route looking, Tata?"

"We going to be connected with each other through the ear piece. I'm going to be hearing your count down. When you get to one minute, I'm pulling up in front of the store. You come out, hop in the truck. We bend a few corners, ditch the truck, and depart in our own, separate vehicles," Tata stated nonchalantly, not even looking at Rico. She played with the toe ring that was on her foot. She was still bent out of shape about what happened at the club, and to find out he had a child on the outside of their relationship.

"Listen, Tata, you don't seem focused. You need to get your shit together. We going live in less than 48 hours."

"Oh I'm focused. Just make sure you on point with your count," Tata said, staring into the eyes of Rico.

He looked like he want to say something hateful, but he just put his smart comment in the back of his throat and moved on. "Alright, we will go over the plan again tonight. Do anyone have a problem with that?"

"No!" everyone said, united.

"Well, good. I got some shit I need to handle," Rico said, pulling the Washington Wizards hat down over his eyes and heading to the door.

"Hey, Jelli, what you getting into?" Tone asked with a sly smile on his face. He'd been trying to get into Jelli's panties for a minute now, but Jelli wasn't feeling him.

"Why? What you got planned?" she asked, batting her eyes seductively.

"I was wondering, could we go grab something to eat?"

"Naw, baby, I'm not hungry. But you can roll with me if you want," Jelli replied.

"Where you going?"

Jelli put a smile on her face. "I'm going to see about a dick."

The girls burst out in laughter. Even Diesel had to laugh at Tone's lame ass.

"Bitch, fuck you!" Tone said, walking out the door behind Rico.

"Jelli, you are dead wrong for that, slim," Diesel said, winking his eye at Tata and walking out the door.

Phatmama and Zoey was on the floor, laughing in tears at how Jelli just played Tone's soft ass.

Tata jumped off her Italian leather sofa and peeked out the blinds to make sure Rico was gone. Seeing his Benz pull out of the driveway with Diesel in it, she went into boss mode. "Alright, bitches, listen up. We hitting Zales at 8:15 a.m. tomorrow. We want to take down the store and be back here before Rico and them do their walkthrough tomorrow. Zoey, what's good with the wheels?" Tata asked.

"Black Audi for the getaway car and two rented Hondas at the switch-up point."

Tata nodded her head in satisfaction. "What about guns and gear, Phatmama?" Tata focused her attention on her second trusted friend.

Phatmama gave up a broad smile as she reached behind the leather sofa she and Tata just shared and introduced a Louis Vuitton luggage bag. She revealed four pink Glock .40s and a bronze-colored Mack-11.

"Damn," Jelli whispered. She never seen a pink gun before. Everything Rico had trained them with had been black or chrome.

All the women grabbed the toy-looking guns. Tata smirked. "This me all day, right here."

"Shit, this is us!" Zoey said, pointing the gun and holding it sideways like she seen in so many gangsta movies. She stood posing in her gangsta stance with a sour apple Blow Pop in her mouth, her face broke down in a mug.

Jelli examined her gun. "I don't know about these, y'all. We go up in there with these pink guns and they might think shit fake and buck on the stick-up."

"Then we make them respect the gun and our gangsta!" Tata said, popping the 30-round extended clip out of the gun and inspecting the high-grade hollow points that rested in the clip.

"And we wearing these," Phatmama stated, holding a Jason-style hockey mask. Zoey admired the mask with a devilish grin on her face, still clutching her pink Glock .40.

Jelli sparked a blunt to calm her nerves. She was apprehensive about the robbery they was gearing up for tomorrow. Even though they'd been planning the heist for a month now, she still wasn't sure they could pull it off without the help of Rico. And if something went wrong, God forbid, and Rico found out, surely he would kill them. She took a heavy pull of the blunt and held the smoke in until the weed smoke burned her lungs. She closed her eyes and slowly let the smoke ease from her lungs.

"So, it seem like everything is ready and set for tomorrow," Tata said, placing the pink Glock back in the Louis Vuitton bag. "I got to ask you this, Phatmama. Where you get the guns from?" Tata asked, pulling her tiny shorts out of the creases of her pussy.

"I'll tell you when the time is right, but you do know I still got my connections from my gun-running days. But I would say all the guns are clean and none traceable," Phatmama said with confidence.

Tata nodded her head in respect to what Phatmama just stated. "Any questions or concerns before tomorrow? Speak on it now or forever hold your clits," Tata said, eyeing the women.

Jelli wanted to say something, but she held her tongue.

"Ok then, ladies, if there's nothing else, I have a youngin' I need to work my mojo on," Tata said, picking up her phone off the black marble table and sending Diesel a text.

***

Pushing the navy blue 600 at a comfortable pace down Suitland Parkway heading into DC, Rico glanced at Diesel, who sat in the passenger seat texting away on his phone. Tapping Diesel's leg and getting his attention, Rico passed him the burning Backwood packed with the loud. Diesel accepted the burning leaf. He inhaled on it as it hung from his lips while he continued to text on his phone.

"You jive-feeling ol' Tata, huh?" Rico asked, never taking his eyes off the road.

"Shit!" Diesel said, dropping the Backwood in his lap by accident from the sudden question Rico threw his way. Diesel snatched the Backwood up off his Polo black label jeans before it could burn a hole in them. He knocked the ashes off his lap. "Damn, Rico, where the fuck that shit come from, slim?" Diesel asked, not looking at his big homie, but watching the scenery as the Benz floated down the parkway.

"Answer the question first, slim," Rico retorted, checking his rearview mirrors.

Diesel swallowed hard and his mouth became dry. "Tata cool people, Rico. I respect her," Diesel said, hitting the Backwood again and letting the smoke seep out of his nose.

"What you know about respecting my bitch? What Tata

done for you to make you respect her?" Rico asked him with a quizzing eye.

"Come on, slim, with all these crazy-ass questions. I respect her because she's your woman, and I respect you. That's why I respect her."

The tension rose a bit in the car. Diesel really wanted to tell Rico if he knew how to treat Tata, he wouldn't be having this conversation with him or worrying about a nigga fucking his bitch.

"You muthafuckin' right, Tata is my bitch. I made the bitch what she is today. When I first met her, she was on lockdown in Hazelton F.C.I., soliciting herself on pen-pal sites for companionship."

Diesel was getting a little attitude at how Rico was trying to downplay and degrade Tata, but he keep his cool.

"I brought that bitch out of Reebok and placed her feet in Fendi, Prada, and Gucci, nigga," Rico said, getting a little too loud for Diesel's liking.

Rico snatched the Backwood out of Diesel's hand. Diesel looked at his mentor with fire in his eyes. "Rico, you trippin', slim."

"I seen how you was eye-fucking Tata back at the house, and how she was fighting to avoid making eye contact with you," Rico said, knocking ashes in the ashtray.

Diesel's heart started to race. Maybe Rico was hip to him and Tata creeping around. "Bruh, you all the way wrong, slim, to think or say some shit like that outta your mouth," Diesel stated, shifting in his seat.

Rico looked at Diesel for a very long time without saying a word. The silence was killing Diesel.

"Don't let Tata trick you to betray me. She's an evil bitch who pack an evil mind." Rico looked over at Diesel. Diesel failed to make eye contact with Rico. "Remember this, Diesel,"

Rico said, switching lanes. "It was a bitch that brought the Romans to their knees and caused them to lose their empire. Many niggas have lost their lives behind a bitch like Tata. Don't be like those who have," Rico said, hitting the Backwood and turning the volume up, letting Shy Glizzy's new single "Blur" beat through the Benz's speakers, hoping Diesel heeded the warning he was giving him.

Jibril Williams

Chapter 7

Tata tossed and turned all night. She could not get more than two hours' worth of sleep, yet she was wide awake like she just drank two Five Hour Energy drinks back-to-back. She scrubbed her body down with hospital disinfectant soap. This was something Rico had taught her and the girls when doing their training. When pulling off a heist, they were not allow to wear makeup, nail polish, eye contacts, or eyelashes. Nothing could be worn that could be linked back to them.

Tata stepped out of the shower and dried off thoroughly with her Polo towel. There was no need to apply any lotion or cosmetics to her skin, but she would be damned if she was going to leave the house without putting any deodorant on. She applied two swipes of her Dove deodorant under each arm. She then stepped into her pecan-brown Donna Karen pinstriped pantsuit. She eased her size-six feet into her white Red Bottoms.

Tata double-checked the clock on the bedroom wall and seen it was 7:05 a.m., and she had 55 minutes to make the commute to her clique's meeting point. Rico made shit way too easy to get out of the house this early in the morning since he didn't have the decency to bring his dog-ass home last night.

Tata grabbed her Gucci knapsack and hit the door.

Sixty minutes later, Tata, Phatmama, Zoey, and Jelli sat in the stolen Audi R8 a block away from the Zales on 15th and Connecticut Avenue. The morning traffic was light. The everyday corporate world people breezed past the Audi as if the car and its occupants was nonexistent. Dressed in black dickies, jumpers, and wearing black latex gloves, the women sat in silence. The only thing that could be heard was the rapid thumping of their heartbeats.

Tata's stomach felt bubbly. She turned around and faced

Zoey and Jelli, who was sitting in the back of the Audi. "You bitches ready?" Tata asked, checking their eyes to see if they were just as afraid as she was.

"Let's do it!" Zoey said, pulling a cherry flavored Blow Pop out of her mouth and cocking a bullet into the chamber of her pink Glock .40. Jelli nodded her head up and down.

"Phatmama, let's hit it," Tata instructed, cocking her own pink Glock.

Phatmama whipped the car into traffic and pulled right up in front of Zales at 8:15 on the nose. Tata's white Red Bottoms struck the pavement. Zoey's yellow Red Bottoms struck out right behind her.

Jelli froze.

Phatmama seen Jelli's hesitation. "Jelli, get your ass out this fucking car."

"No!" Jelli replied.

"Bitch! You got one second to move or I'm spilling your brains on that back window," Phatmama said, pointing her Glock in Jelli's face.

Jelli looked at the backs of Tata and Zoey entering Zales, and back at the gun pointing in her face. She sucked her teeth, pulled her hockey mask over her face, and jumped out of the Audi and sprinted into the store behind Tata and Zoey. Her powder-blue Red Bottoms click-clacked along the way.

Phatmama pulled off.

"Let's get it, everybody. I need all you fuckas' hands up in the air where I can see 'em," Tata came into the Zales screaming, weaving her Pink Glock with the 30-round extender hanging from it. Only three customers resided in the store. The two clerks were on the floor helping two of the customers.

The store went into a small panic seeing the three robbers rush the store, demanding their hands in the air. A tall, slim blond clerk placed her hands in the air and closed her eyes. She was so petrified seeing the hockey masks. It made her think about the masked murderer that killed everyone in the movie *Friday the 13th*. She just knew she was going to be killed.

Jelli and Zoey went to work breaking the glass on the display cases and removing tray after tray of the store's precious merchandise. "Three minutes!" Tata yelled out, still keeping her eyes and gun trained on the store hostages.

"I can do this," Jelli mumbled to herself behind her mask as she stuffed the jewelry into the Gucci knapsack. Zoey moved from one display case to the other with confidence and the skill of a professional.

The white, bald headed Zales manager eased himself toward the counter and inched his arm down to his side, trying to activate the silent alarm. He really didn't believe the robbers' pink guns were real. Easing his hand down toward the silent alarm–

Boom! The pink Glock in Tata's hand let off a deadly roar. "Bitch, get your fucking hands up!" Tata screamed, pointing the smoking gun at the manager. "Don't let me tell you again! The next one is going to knock your brains loose. Now, try me!"

A hollow-point slammed into the cash register, leaving it shattered. The manager shot his hands in the air. The shot from the gun now had his legs trembling hard.

The shot made Jelli look up. Zoey kept dumping the jewelry in the bag.

"Two minutes!" Tata informed. "Keep loading the bag, Blue," Tata spoke to Jelli, calling her 'Blue' based on the powder-blue Red Bottoms she wore.

Jelli snapped out of her daze.

"One minute," Tata announced. She was feeling good that she was down to her last minute.

"Done!" Zoey yelled out.

"Done!" Jelli yelled out also.

"*Mami,* come get us!" Tata spoke through her earpiece.

"En route," came back through the piece. In a matter of seconds, Phatmama was pulling up in front of the Zales. Zoey put her hand on the door handle of the store, getting ready to make her was out of the store.

"Wait!" Tata yelled, stopping her. "The diamond cart." Tata snatched the knapsack from Jelli and hopped the counter where the diamond cart was located.

"Come on, White, leave it," Zoey yelled in a panic. She knew they was going against protocol by staying in the store longer than they were supposed to.

Tata ignored Zoey.

"Move, bitch!" Tata said, pointing the Glock at the manager's head. The cracka muthafucka dropped to the floor and balled into a fetal position. Tata shook her head at the store manager, opened the diamond cart door, and unloaded its valuables into the knapsack in a matter of seconds.

Tata hopped back over the counter and made her exit behind Zoey. Jelli brought up the rear, their Red Bottoms click-clacking in the process.

***

"We did it! We did it!" Tata and Zoey jumped up and down like they just won the WNBA championship for the Washington Mystics.

Laying on the black marble table were four Rolexes, two white gold Daytonas with diamond bezels and an Oyster Perpetual Air-King. This was the latest model of the Rolex, with a starting cost of $50,000. The Cartier selection they snatched was five Parsha Cartiers with the emerald dial on them, which came with a pretty price tag. The medium Tank Anglaise was Tata's favorite. The table also held 12 diamond tennis bracelets with varying colors of diamonds in them, which made Tata's black marble table look like it was made out of multicolored jellybeans. And that was the tip of the iceberg, because the rings and diamond bangles were flawless, and Tata still hadn't finished emptying the knapsack.

Tata and Zoey were still celebrating until Tata caught the stare down that was going on between Jelli and Phatmama. "What the fuck up with you bitches?" Tata asked, stopping her happy dance and addressing her friends.

"This big-boned-ass bitch pointed her fucking gun in my face," Jelli said, breaking eye contact with Phatmama.

"Yeah, and this scaredy-ass bitch was going to leave you and Zoey to pull the heist off by y'all self. The move was a three-woman job, and I had to put my gun in her face to get her ass out the fucking car," Phatmama retorted with malice in her voice.

"Is that true, Jelli?" Tata asked, looking at Jelli with a little glint of disappointment in her voice.

"A bitch got cold feet, but I handled my business, so that shouldn't be a factor in this conversation."

"This bitch is lying through her fucking teeth. I told her to get out the car, and she told me no until I put that gun in her face," Phatmama replied, mugging on Jelli.

"I'm not going to be too many bitches," Jelli spat, trying to take the focus off the fact she was going to leave her friends at the most critical time of their life.

Phatmama turned her head to the side like a pit would do when something had caught its focus. "Jelli, you know I love you like a sister, but I'll give that ass a head-up fade."

"Then lets run it, bitch," Jelli said, jumping up off the sofa and kicking her powder blue Red Bottoms off her feet. Phatmama followed suit by kicking her Red Bottoms off.

"Naw, y'all, don't fight!" Zoey cried out.

"Naw, let them go. Let's put this shit up real quick," Tata said, scooping the jewelry off the marble table into one of the knapsacks and tossing it in the closet by the front door. Tata grabbed a Backwood off the table and followed Jelli and Phatmama to the backyard.

As soon as their feet hit the grass of Tata's backyard, Jelli and Phatmama went at it like heavyweights. Phatmama threw a wild haymaker, which Jelli easily ducked, catching Phatmama in the gut with a right hook. "Ugh!" Phatmama grunted from the contact of Jelli's punch. But Phatmama recovered quickly and shot her jab, making it connect with Jelli's head, making her stumble back on her heels.

A knot started to formulate on Jelli's forehead. Jelli charged Phatmama, swinging her elbow, catching Phatmama on the cheekbone under her eye and giving her an equal-sized knot to match the one Phatmama placed on her forehead.

Tata and Zoey sat on the steps of the back porch, smoking the Backwood and watching Jelli and Phatmama go at it. It hurt Tata to watch her two best friends go at it like that, but she knew sometimes a good fight between one another would strengthen the bond between friends. War had a funny way of bringing people together or tearing them apart She just hoped this was going to be one of them situations where the friendship would outweigh the war.

Jelli was no stranger to combat. She grew up in the streets of Clayton, Georgia. When a woman was fine and juicy as Jelli was, she had to learn to hold her own, because bitches stayed hella jealous of her and the attention she got from their men.

The Army made Phatmama tough as nails. Combat training made her a force not to be fucked with.

Jelli grabbed Phatmama's hair. Phatmama knew Jelli was fighting dirty, so she grabbed ahold of Jelli's neck and pushed her thumbs into the pressure points. "Argh!" Jelli jerked out of

Phatmama's grasp.

"That's enough!" Tata yelled out, stepping in between the two women.

Phatmama and Jelli looked like they wanted to ignore Tata's demand. Tata and Zoey stepped between Jelli and Phatmama. Both of the women's chests rose and fell. Both held matching vehemence in their eyes. Jelli stood there with a ripped shirt and a juicy breast exposed.

"You bitches good?" Tata asked.

Both women hesitated to respond. Neither wanted to be the first one to admit they had enough.

Phatmama reluctantly nodded her head up and down, signaling she was good. Jelli did the same.

"A'ight! Dap it up," Tata said, stepping from between Jelli and Phatmama.

The two women stepped in and embraced each other, giving a sisterly hug. They then applied their special handshake to signify they was sisters.

"Sorry for putting that heat in your face. I'm dead wrong for that," Phatmama confessed.

"I'm sorry for freezing up when my girls needed me the most," Jelli retorted with water in her eyes.

"Let this be the last time a member of this sisterhood raises a hand to one another," Tata spoke, letting smoke seep from her nose and mouth as she talked. Zoey stood there, nodding her head up and down in agreement on what Tata was speaking. "From this day forth, our motto is: If one ride, we all roll. If one hesitate, then we all motivate. And if one betrays, then know God forgives, and we don't," Tata said, looking into the eyes of her closest confidants. They all took in the seriousness in Tata's words. "Today is a new beginning for us. No more depending on a nigga to provide and take care of us. From now on we make our own moves. We march to the rhythm of our own drumbeat," Tata continued giving her girls the talk that would unite them. She hit the Backwood again and passed it to Phatmama. "Together, we can survive any storm," Tata said, placing her hands behind her back. "But solo, we will certainly wither and die. Our next move–"

"Tata, get the fuck in here!" Rico yelled from the back door of the house.

"Shit!" Tata mumbled under her breath. She walked toward a waiting Rico, her clique followed behind her.

Rico stood there, holding the door open for the group of women. As each woman passed Rico and entered the house, he inspected their faces and body language. Jelli walked past Rico, not making eye contact with him while holding her shirt together, trying hard to conceal the luscious breast Phatmama had ripped out of her shirt. Phatmama was the only one out of the four who made direct eye contact with Rico. She mugged him hard, and he returned the look. He still was bitter with her for putting that blade to his neck at the club.

Tata's heart was beating harder than a set of drums at a Go-go concert. She was hoping Rico didn't find the bag of jewelry she had recklessly stashed in the hallway closet.

"What the fuck you muthafuckas been up to this morning? And Tata, before your ass lie to me, the hood of your truck is still warm, and by the way you all are dressing, you all been somewhere," Rico said, noticing Tata's Donna Karen attire, Phatmama's Prada business suit, Zoey's white halter dress with the powder-blue Red Bottoms and Jelli's Jimmy Choo pants and ripped blouse.

"Rico, *papi*, what are you tripping on? We only went into the city to meet a realtor that leases buildings. Phatmama finally saved up enough money to open up her own hair salon that she always been dreaming of doing," Tata said.

"So you bitches don't know nothing about this right here?

Alexa, turn the TV on to Fox News," Rico ordered the Google electronic box that was connected to every aspect of the 17,000 square-foot home.

"Yes, sir!" Alexa replied, turning the 80-inch Sony smart curve screen TV on to Fox 5. In the blink of an eye, Tata and her girls were staring at a Fox 5 news reporter standing in front of the Zales they robbed not even 45 minutes ago.

"Just at 8:15 this morning, three female robbers entered this Zales jewelry store waving pink guns and wearing Red Bottom heels," the heavyset woman reported. "We received confirmation that the robbers seemed to be professionals. They emptied out every display case the store had in under four minutes. They even got away with the diamond cart jewelry that held nine black diamonds estimated to be worth $40,000 apiece, and that's not even counting the watches, bracelets, and other diamonds the robbers got away with. The owners of the Zales have issued a $100,000 reward for any information that could lead the police to the bandits who robbed the store this morning. Please contact the number on the bottom of the screen. We will keep you updated on this terrible crime. I'm Cynthia Moore with Fox 5 News."

Rico turn and look at the women. "So, y'all don't know nothing about this?" Rico asked, staring and checking everyone's expressions.

"No!" they all answered in unison.

Rico could feel it was some sucka-shit going on, but he couldn't put it together at the moment. He knew Tata didn't have the resources to get rid of the jewelry on her own, and no pawn shop in a three-state radius was going to touch the jewelry because it would be too hot bring too much heat on their establishment. So Rico knew Tata would have to come to him sooner or later. All he would have to do is wait her out.

"Start casing the next job. I want the details in two weeks,"

Rico said, walking out of the house and burning some rubber out of the driveway as he pulled off in his Benz.

Tata ran to the closet and returned with the knapsack. She dumped all the jewelry on the floor, and a small, black velvet bag hit her feet. She snatched the velvet bag up and opened it with trembling hands.

Nine flawless diamonds fell into her palm.

Tata smiled. "Damn. This what $360,000 feels like."

Chapter 8

"Man, I'm telling you, Tata and them bitches pulled the Zales robbery," Rico stated, knocking back a shot of Hennessey Black. "Man, look at them," Rico said, pointing to the TV that showed actual footage of the robbery. The news had been showing the footage over and over for the last hour.

"Rico, I can't tell how you can tell. Them muthafuckas there got gold wigs and masks on. Plus their jumpsuits are too damn baggie to tell their figures apart from one another," Tone said, pouring himself a drink and refilling Rico's glass.

"Plus, Rico, the way the heist took place isn't how we trained Tata and them. When we go in the stores, we make every bitch in that muthafucka hit the floor face down. But what I see here, they let everyone stay standing and just place their hands in the air," Diesel said as he broke buds up and placed them in the cherry-flavored Backwood.

"I know that, slim, but that was a rookie move on their part," Rico retorted.

"Okay, if that's the case, then how they going to get off the merchandise?" Diesel asked.

"I don't know, slim, but maybe you can tell me, being that you are so fond of Tata."

Diesel looked up from his Backwood twisting. "Come on, Rico, you still on that bullshit?" Diesel asked with his face distorted.

Rico pulled his chrome Colt .45 with the red diamond-encrusted handle from his hip and shoved it in Diesel's face. "Where the fuck you was at this morning?"

Diesel didn't flinch. He stared at Rico with murder in his eyes as if Rico asked him to suck his dick or something.

"Huh? Nigga where was you? Did you help them bitches?" Rico asked through clenched teeth.

"Naw, slim, I didn't help them bitches do nothing, and I was at the crib this morning, waiting on you to call me so we could do the walk-through we had scheduled this morning," Diesel said, breathing deeply through his nose.

"Let me see your phone, nigga," Rico asked, still holding the four-fifth to Diesel's melon.

Diesel swallowed hard. He nodded his head toward his pocket. Rico fished the phone out of his pocket and tried to access the phone, but the phone was locked by a password.

"What's the password, nigga?"

Diesel hesitated.

"Aye, slim, you tripping, Rico. You going to let this shit unhinge you. You acting out of character, and it got you making some bad decisions right now. That's Diesel who you got your burner pointed at," Tone said, trying to talk some sense into Rico's head, before he knocked Diesel's noodles loose.

Rico came to his senses and took Tone's advice, lowering the gun from Diesel's face and throwing his phone in his lap. "Stay the fuck away from Tata," Rico said, walking over to Tone's minibar, pouring himself another shot of Hennessey Black, and downing it.

Diesel jumped to his feet and made his exit. He was wrestling with two emotions: anger and fear. Fear won the battle as soon as he exited Tone's house. He spilled his stomach contents on Tone's front lawn. He was shaken bad. Him and Tata's affair was so close to being exposed if Rico could have gained accessed to his phone and read all the text messages and seen all the sexy pictures he and Tata had been trading with each other.

Tonight was a close call, but Rico made it easy for Diesel to cross him. Rico just signed his death certificate in blood.

Diesel wiped the leftover vomit from the corners of his mouth with the back of his hand while his heart and mind were centered on a deadly betrayal.

***

"No, please, don't do this!" Corporal Tanya Foxx cried.

"Now, Corporal Foxx, I done told you before that every man in this platoon gets the chance to sample them good ol' American goods that rest between them legs of yours," Sergeant Perkins said as he dropped his Army fatigues around his ankles, exposing his thick manhood that curved upward.

Corporal Foxx fought with every bit of strength she had in her, but she wasn't a match for the four platoon members who held her arms and legs down. She screamed at the top of her lungs as Sgt. Perkins positioned himself between her thick thighs and plunged deep into her. She never knew a white man could be that large. Sgt. Perkins stretched her walls to the max.

Corporal Foxx's screams could not be heard in the mountains of Afghanistan. She struggled hard as Sgt. Perkins pumped feverishly in and out of her as the other platoon members cheered him on.

Sweat dripped off his face and onto her naked body. For every thrust Sgt. Perkins gave her, it felt like he ripped her more with every stroke.

"Ahh!"

Phatmama jolted from her nightmare in a cold sweat. The thin t-shirt that covered her body was drenched in perspiration. She was breathing heavily. She sat up in her bed, planted her bare feet on the floor, and placed her head in the palms of her hands. She cried softly.

It had been 12 long years, and Sgt. Perkins haunted her to this very day. She still could feel his touch and the stale smell of cigarettes that hung on his breath like the strong odor of a ho's pussy that had been fucking on the track all night. Every image of every platoon member who ever climbed on top of her and invaded her body as if she was anything less than a human was forever embedded in Phatmama's memory.

"Ugh!" cried Phatmama. She hated that she could not get the terrible events out of her mind. Being in the Army indeed had made her tough, but it also took something away from her. She didn't know what it was that died in her in the mountains of Afghanistan. All she knew was she felt empty inside and needed to rid the world of men like Sgt. Perkins, or any man who only saw women as something to abuse or control and dump their sexual loads into.

Phatmama got off the bed and removed her soaked shirt, placing it in the bathroom hamper. She took a quick shower, stepped out, and halfway dried herself off. She fired up the half-smoked blunt that sat next to her bed in an ashtray. "This what a bitch need, right here," Phatmama spoke out loud to herself, taking a long pull of the blunt.

She picked up her Gucci designer watch and seen it was 1:22 a.m., and she knew sleep was out of the question. She hit the power button on the Sony remote, bringing the 60-inch flat screen to life. Porn stars Buns4ever and Pinky entertained each other in the 69 position.

Phatmama laid back on her bed, getting an eyeful of the two porn stars feasting upon each other's pussies. Phatmama opened her legs wide and played with the soft, moist flesh on her clit. She bit down on her lip.

Reaching over and grabbing her phone, she found Rocco's number in her contacts. The phone rang twice and a deep baritone voice came through.

"Hello."

"Mm! Rocco!" Phatmama's moans came through the phone.

"What it do, Phatmama?" Rocco said in a sexy tone, knowing Phatmama called for some late-night phone sex.

"Oh! Rocco, she's so wet!" Phatmama moaned and pushed two fingers in and out of her wet box.

"Baby, let me come scoop you up and bring you back to my place so I can see how wet that thang really is."

Phatmama hung up in Rocco's ear, and moments later his phone rang, indicating someone was Facetiming him. Rocco hit accept on his phone and was greeted by Phatmama's two fingers gliding in and out of her pussy. The whole time Buns4ever and Pinky was what really had Phatmama on fire and dripping wet.

"Damn, Phatmama," Rocco whispered. He was dying to fuck Phatmama. A few weeks ago he had the privilege of cooking her some dinner at his house. He wined and dined her, but was disappointed at the end of the night to find out Phatmama was on her monthly period, but he got some slow neck from her and sent her ass home in an Uber with sore jaw muscles and a stomach full of high-protein nut. He had a policy he lived by: if a bitch don't fuck, then she don't spend the night at his place. Phatmama wasn't really his type. She was on the chunky side, but it was something about her that drew him to her like a moth to a flame.

"You like what you see, Rocco?" Phatmama asked as her face appeared on the screen of the phone.

"Ain't no muthafuckin' question!" Rocco replied, showing his pearly whites.

"Well, you can see all of this next week when I'm free. Oh, hold on, Rocco! I'm cumming!" Phatmama screamed out, turning the phone back to her pussy. Phatmama worked her two fingers in and out of her pussy while she rotated her thumb around her clit. "Oh shit, Rocco!" Phatmama moaned and squirted her juices all over the screen of the phone.

The scene excited Rocco. He had never seen a woman squirt. He only heard about certain women who had the ability to perform the rare gift.

The screen of his phone went blank. The show Phatmama just gave him had him fucked up. All he could do was pull out his dick and stroke away.

***

"I'm telling you, Tata, that nigga knows we are fucking around," Diesel said, lying naked on the "W" Hotel bed.

"Diesel, that nigga don't know shit! If he did, he would have jumped on my ass by now and bodied your ass," Tata stated as she came from out of the bathroom naked.

"I hear what you are saying, but that nigga got something up his sleeve. He thinks you and the girls pulled the Zales robbery off." Diesel grabbed ahold of his manhood and slowly started stroking it.

"Listen, Diesel, Rico is just paranoid, thinking that someone is going to steal me away from him. And he's tripping because I haven't gave that nigga no pussy since we started fucking. And for the Zales robbery, I wish I did pull that shit off so I could get the fuck away from Rico sorry ass and be with who I really love and who loves me," Tata said, poking out her big, luscious lips.

"And who is that who loves you?" Diesel inquired.

Tata gave him a smile and gently touched Diesel's chiseled chest. "It's you, daddy, who really love me."

"That's right. I almost killed that nigga tonight about you," Diesel boasted, lying like a bitch.

Nigga, whatever! Tata said in her mind. "If it came down to it, do you think you could handle Rico?"

"Yeah, I could handle Rico with no problem, but we need to come up with a plan to dead this nigga, because I'm not going to keep being around this nigga and fucking you at the same time."

"I feel what you are saying, Diesel. Let me think of something, and I will get with you on that," Tata said, straddling his semi-erect penis. "But for right now, make love to me, Diesel, before I got to go home to that weak-ass nigga.

"Oh, I will! I'm going to send you home with a swollen pussy."

Chapter 9

"I'm working on exchanging the goods for cash," Tata said, passing the Backwood to Jelli.

"So, you telling us we robbed Zales, and we can't cash in on the jewels we took?" Zoey stated, looking at Tata crazy.

Jelli was too vexed about the revelation to even comment on it. She just accepted the loud pack from Tata and inhaled it deeply.

"How long it's going to take for you to make that happen?" Phatmama questioned.

"Probably about another 30 days, at least."

"Shit!" Phatmama retorted, even though she wasn't hurting for no money. The money she hit Bless for had her with a nice stash.

"But in the meantime, we need to pull off another lick. Something we can get a direct cash flow from. Nothing we have to exchange merchandise for cash. Do anybody have any ideas?" Tata asked.

"Well, I might, but I need a week to set it up, though," Phatmama replied.

"What it is?" Jelli chimed in. She wasn't ready to take on anything like a bank or some shit like that.

"The check cashing place on 14th Street. The small one that sit next door to the empty building we went to look at about six months ago about renting it to open the salon."

"Yeah, I remember. I think we could take the place. How much do you think we could get out of there?" Jelli said, tapping ashes into the ashtray that sat on her lap.

"Maybe 70 to 100 thousand, easily," Phatmama stated.

"Put it together, ASAP!" Tata informed Phatmama.

"Are we going to steal the Helzog heist from under Rico?" Zoey asked, rolling her eyes at Jelli for being a Hoover on her

Backwood. "Jelli, pass that shit."

Jelli sucked her teeth and blew smoke in Zoey's face when she passed the weed to her. Phatmama giggled at her weed-loving friends.

"Naw, I don't think we are ready for a job in Pentagon city," Tata replied. "We going to let Rico and them take Helzog. We'll just play our normal roles and drive the getaway cars." Tata stood up to leave. "So, everyone just chill and remain normal and stay out of trouble. I'm getting ready to head home. I have some shit I need to take care of at the home front."

"How could you ever call a place home where you're not happy at?" Phatmama stated with concern and a hint of disdain in her voice.

"It's okay temporarily, *mami*," Tata assured Phatmama.

Tata shook it up with her girls in their signature handshake and bounced.

***

Two hours later, Tata pulled up to her Temple Hills home and climbed out of her Acura truck, grabbing the bags out of the back seat. She was on a mission to put Rico's suspicions to rest about the Zales heist, but most of all she wanted to dead the seed he had planted in his head about her and Diesel.

Tata walked to the front door to find an Amazon delivery box waiting on her. "What the fuck?" Tata looking strangely at the box until she remembered she had ordered the books *Blood Stains of A Shotta 1-3* by Jamaica and *Lipstick Killa* by MiMi. She couldn't wait to take a long, hot bath, sip on some Moscato, and get lost in the pages of one of those books.

Where is Ski? She should have been here to sign for the package, Tata thought to herself.

Tata opened the door and, due to her hands being full, she

scooted the Amazon box through the door with the help of her foot. The house was silent.

Kicking her black Red Bottoms off at the door, Tata made her way to the kitchen to put away the groceries and start preparing dinner for Rico.

Hearing what could be a moan, Tata's body froze, trying to see if her ears was deceiving her. "Mm!" she heard it again.

"What the hell?" Tata said, closing the cabinets and tiptoeing up the stairs, where the noise was coming from.

"Mm! Uh! Uh!"

Tata could hear the moaning more clearly, and it was coming from her bedroom. "I know this nigga ain't fucking another bitch in our bed," Tata said, spinning on her heels and going back downstairs to retrieve the Glock 19 out of her Gucci bag. Tata never left home without the weapon.

She cocked the gun like a professional would and tiptoed back upstairs to catch a cheating-ass Rico. "I'm going to body both of these bitches," Tata mumbled, creeping up the stairs.

"Oh, yes! Oh, yes! Deeper!" the woman cried out in pleasure. Tata could hear the woman more vividly.

When she broke the threshold of the bedroom door, her jaw dropped like it weighed a ton. Then it curled into a frown. She stepped back out into the hallway before she could be seen. She tucked the gun into the small of her back and removed her leather Louis Vuitton belt, then charged into the room, surprising the couple.

"You li'l nasty-ass bitch, gonna fuck in my bed?" Tata screamed, scaring the shit out of her niece Ski and a boy she often seen washing a new Lexus in a driveway a few houses down from hers. The boy lay naked on top of Ski, his naked body pumping away.

Whap! Whap! Tata brought her belt down on top of their bodies.

"Argh!" the boy hollered.

"Auntie, I'm sorry!" Ski cried out, trying to shield herself from Tata's wrath, but it was too much skin for Tata to attack.

Whap! Whap! Whap! Tata's belt cut through the air and bit down into Ski's breast.

"Ouch!" Ski yapped.

"I can't believe you would do some shit like this!" *Whap!* Tata brought the belt down on Ski's legs.

Tata looked at the boy and saw he was a little older than Ski. Her eyes dropped down to his glistening penis and she got madder. "You in here raw-doggin' my niece?" Tata went H.A.M. on his ass. *Whap! Whap! Whap! Whap!* "You don't even have the fucking decency to put a fucking condom on your dick?" Tata delivered another blow. *Whap!*

The boy ducked Tata's belt by an inch. He drew his hand back like he was going to smack the shit out of Tata, but Tata was quick on the draw. She upped the Glock quickly and pointing it at him. "I wish the fuck you would."

The boy's arm froze in midair and he swallow hard, but he was unfazed by the gun. That told Tata he had a little street in him and had been under pressure like this before.

"Get the fuck out my house," Tata said, still pointing the gun at him.

The boy couldn't move fast enough. He jumped in his Tom Ford jeans in a split second and stuffed his feet into his Jordans without tying them up. He snatched his shirt off the floor and hauled ass without even looking back at Ski.

Tata stood over Ski's naked body as she lay there on the bed, trembling in fear. Tata drew her arm back to give her niece a few more licks, but something stopped her. "Ski, go get your ass in the shower, then pull these sheets off this bed and put them in the washer."

Ski came out her fetal position, covering her womanly-sized

breasts, and made her was past Tata.

Tata fastened her Louis Vuitton belt back around her waist and tucked her gun in the small of her back, shaking her head at the thought of her niece fucking in her house and in her bed. What was puzzling to Tata was how her niece was taking all that dick like a grown-ass woman. The young boy was working with a monster. Tina definitely had to have a conversation with Ski.

I can't believe this little bitch was fucking in my house, Tata though to herself as she went back downstairs to finish preparing dinner for Rico.

***

Tata had just lit the candles and sat them in the middle of the cherry oak wood dinner table. Rico called and told her he would be pulling up in 20 minutes, so she had just enough time to check on the chicken Alfredo that was stewing on top of the stove and double check the steamed broccoli and rice. She knew Rico hated crunchy broccoli, so she plucked one of the broccoli stems out and sampled it for texture. "Perfect!" Tata mumbled, sucking the broccoli juices from her fingers.

She heard keys turning in the front door, which made her check her outfit once and strut to meet Rico.

Rico walked through the door and saw Tata standing there in her Next Top Model stance, which would have made Tyra Banks proud of her. "Damn!" he whispered. The chocolate beauty stood in front of him wearing a pair of form-fitting, light gray Chanel slacks. The pants clung to her thighs and deeply cut into her private area, letting the crotch of her pants take the full shape of her pussy. Standing a few inches taller in her four-inch Jimmy Choo stilettoes, Rico took the view in and loved everything he was seeing. His eyes stopped at her black Chanel blouse that damn near exposed Tata's double-B cups.

Rico licked his lips. "Damn, *mami*, what's the occasion?" he asked with a sly grin on his face and lust in his eyes.

"Well, come and find out," Tata said, grabbing his hand and escorting him to the dinner table.

The whole time Rico's eyes was on Tata's round backside. Her ass jumped and banged together with every step. Rico wondered if she had on any drawers.

Tata knew Rico was watching her ass, so she put a little extra in her walk.

Rico seen the candlelight flickering and the dinner table set for two. He figured something was up.

"Have a seat, *papi*, while I go get the food." Tata kissed Rico's lips and gave him a little tongue in the process. She wasn't ready to mess up her MAC lip-gloss just yet.

Rico sat down and made himself comfortable. He wondered if she was going to come clean about her and them ungrateful bitches stepping on his toes and robbing the Zales without him. *Stupid-ass bitches can't even get rid of the fucking goods. Yeah, them bitches must need me. That's what all this shit is about,* Rico thought to himself.

Tata came out of the kitchen carrying two plates. "Here you go, *papi*. Your favorite," Tata said, setting a plate in front of him. "Chicken Alfredo, white rice, and steamed broccoli with cheese. And I also have two types of desserts for you. One is a blueberry cheesecake, but the other dessert you gonna have to wait until later to find out what that is," Tata stated with a little sexual undertone in her voice.

"You know, *mami*, when it comes to dessert, I'm like a kid. I'm greedy as fuck!" Rico said, looking Tata dead in her eyes.

"Well, good, I have so much of it you can eat as much as you like," Tata said, smiling and returning Rico's stare.

The knock on the door interrupted their flow. "Oh, shit! I

forgot Tina was coming to pick that fast-ass daughter of hers up. I been so busy cooking I forgot," Tata said, getting up from the table.

"Ski here?" Rico questioned.

"Yeah, she's upstairs. I told her I didn't want to see her ass until her mother came to get her." Tata walked to the door to let Tina in. "What's good with your pregnant ass?" Tata spoke as she opened the door for Tina and kissed her on the cheek.

"Ain't shit, just knocked the fuck up! I'm three months and I'm showing already, and my feet are already starting to swell and my ass started to spread, but that's a good thing," Tina smiled, rubbing her hands over her butt. "But shit wasn't like this when I was pregnant with Ski. That's how I know I'm carrying a badass little boy. I can't–" Tina stopped talking once she saw Rico sitting at the dinner table enjoying a plate of food like he didn't have a care in the world. She gave him the evil eye as she placed her hand on her stomach. She suddenly started to feel sick.

"You need to have a serious talk with Ski or she's going to be walking around here pregnant like you," Tata stated to Tina as she went to the first step of the stairs. "Ski, get your ass down here. Your mom is here."

All Tina heard when Tata was talking was, "Blah-blah-blah-blah-blah-blah-blah." Tina was focused on Rico.

Rico paid Tina no mind. He kept his head down and enjoyed his food.

"Tina, did you hear what I just said?"

"Huh? Oh, what?" Tina replied, taking her eyes off Rico for the first time.

"I said I caught Ski fucking in my bed with that young nigga that lives down the street with the good hair."

Tina balled her face up. "Ski, get the fuck down here." Tina wasn't mad about Ski having sex. She knew her daughter became sexually active at the age of 13, but fucking in someone else's bed was a no-no.

Ski came downstairs with her shoulders hunched over and her eyes cast downward. Tears stained her cheeks as she stopped in front of her mother.

Tina's nose flared in and out. "So, you having sex in other people's beds, huh?" Tina questioned her daughter, but before Ski could answer her mother, Tata interrupted.

"No, she wasn't having sex! She was straight fucking like a grown-ass woman, 'specially according to what I witnessed today."

Rico let out a chuckle.

"And she was fucking without protection, so the young nigga was raw-dogging it," Tata said with a disgusted look on her face.

"Girl, what the fuck is wrong with you?" Tina snatched Ski up by her shirt and got in her face.

"It's no need for that. I wore that ass out with my Louie V belt."

"Tsh!" Tina sucked her teeth and rolled her eyes. "Get the fuck out my face and go wait in the truck. We talking about this shit when we get home." Tina focusing her attention back on Tata and Rico. "Well, I see you two are all booed up and spending some one-on-one time with each other."

Tata caught Tina's hint of sarcasm in her voice, but she didn't say anything. She thought Tina was still mad about the situation that took place at the club with Rico. "Yeah, we are trying to reconnect, but do you want me to fix you and Ski a plate to take with you?" Tata asked.

"Naw, *mami,* we good. We going to hit the KFC before we get to the house."

"Well then, bitch, let me get back to my man," Tata said with a smile.

Tina rolled her eyes and stormed out of the dining room and front door without saying goodbye. "Damn, someone got a fat dildo stuck up their ass," Tata said, chalking her sister's behavior up as being of an emotional pregnant woman.

"Tata, you're straight crazy," Rico said, scooping a forkful of rice and chicken and shoving it into his mouth. "Mm, *mami,* this is so good. You put your foot in this."

Tata smiled and took a sip of her red wine. "Alexa! Play the playlist I have set for tonight."

Ella Mai song *Boo'd Up* started playing through the surround sound. Tata began to rock in her chair to the music. She closed her eyes and sang a few bars with Ella Mai.

"Feelings, so deep in my feelings.
No, this ain't really like me.
Can't control my anxiety.
Feeling like I'm touching the ceiling.
When I'm with you I can't breath.
Boy, you do something to me."

Tata opened her eyes and caught Rico intensely watching the sway of her body. She sexually and bashfully smiled at him.

It was moments like this that he adored Tata the most, the super sexy beauty from Miami Gardens, South Florida. His conscience started to weigh on him. He felt like shit for how he'd been treating Tata lately. He sat his fork down, reached over, and placed his hand on top of hers.

"*Mami*, I need to apologize to you. I'm sorry for all the bullshit I been taking you through. A nigga hasn't been himself, and I been stressing about all kinds of shit, and I been taking my anger out on you."

Tata looked at Rico's features and seen sincerity on his face, and if she didn't know any better and the fact he had a whole baby outside of their relationship he hadn't even told her about yet, she would have believed the words coming out of his mouth.

"Shh! Baby, please, that's water under the bridge," Tata said, holding a finger up to Rico's lips, stopping him from talking.

"Naw, *mami,* we haven't even addressed the situation that took place at the club a month ago."

"Rico, baby, that's behind us. Let's not dwell on the past. Like I said, that's water under the bridge," Tata retorted and leaned over and kissed Rico's lips, this time giving him so much tongue. Rico sucked on her bottom lip so tenderly and passionately. Tata loved when her lips was closely paid attention to.

She pulled away from Rico. "You know what, baby? Let's skip dinner and go straight to the second desert, because my cream pie is full of cream," Tata said, standing up and letting Rico see the wet spot that started to formulate at the crotch of her pants.

Rico stood up and made Tata step out of her Jimmy Choos and drop her pants to her ankles. She stepped out of them also, leaving her standing in front of Rico with nothing on except her black Chanel blouse. Rico found out his earlier assumption that Tata was panty less was true.

Rico sampled Tata's lips again, but this time he kissed her with hunger, sucking and biting on her tongue.

Tata tried to unbuckle his Polo jeans, but Rico knocked her hands away. He let his hands travel up to Tata's blouse and expose the softness of her ripe melons by pulling her breast overtop of her blouse. He pulled and sucked on her Tootsie Roll-sized nipples and enjoying her taste.

Tata's body was overheating. Her juices leaked down her inner thigh. Rico dropped a hand between her legs. The wet, gushy sound he encountered when he pushed his middle finger inside of her made him want to drink from her cup of love, despite the suspicion he had of her and Diesel. He couldn't really see Tata giving a young nigga like Diesel the pleasure of laying pipe to her.

Rico pushed his plate out of the way and replaced it with Tata's ass cheeks. He sat down in his chair right between Tata's chocolate thighs. Her glazed-over pussy lips stared back at him. Boy, did Tata have a phat pussy on her. Rico devilishly grinned, grabbed a cloth napkin from the table and tide it around his neck like a baby bib, and bowed his head in prayer.

Tata looked at him strangely. "*Papi*, what are you doing?"

Rico lifted his head from prayer. "I'm ready for the dessert. I had to say my grace, now I'm ready to put my face in the place," Rico stated, diving tongue-first into Tata's cream pie.

Jibril Williams

Chapter 10

"Are you going to let me stay the night this time?" Phatmama asked.

"You going to let a nigga fuck in every hole?" Rocco shot back, running a hand over his goatee and holding a silly smirk on his face.

"You know what? If I didn't like you so damn much, I would be offended at your comment, but I'll tell you what. If you can get me open and work that dick like a real savage nigga supposed to, you can have any hole you want," Phatmama said, playing with Rocco's ego.

"Like a real savage nigga suppose to! You never had a real one like me, so you are in for a treat. And from what I remember you telling me, you said you was close-built and you couldn't take no dick."

Phatmama fell over in laughter behind the wheel of her Navigator truck. Rocco turned his head sideways and smiled with his arm resting on the trucks doorframe.

"Ok, bae, you got a bitch," Phatmama said, showing all 32 teeth. "So, if I let you smash, can you promise you would be gentle with me?" Phatmama asked in her little kid voice.

"Yeah, I promise I will take my time with it."

Phatmama could tell Rocco was lying. Niggas liked to put that hammer down on a bitch when they found out they couldn't take that D, but she had a trick for that ass, though. "Ok, then. Let's go."

"We can do this, but you know the drill," Rocco stated, sticking his hand out.

Phatmama powered off her phone and placed it in Rocco's hand. Rocco was a semi-cautious dude. Taking the phone from Phatmama assured him she couldn't call or take pictures to remember where his crib was located. He wasn't really tripping too much about bringing Phatmama to his house because he was making preparations to move in the next few weeks.

Rocco walked away, hopped in his smoke-gray 550 Benz, and moved out with Phatmama right behind him, heading over the 14th Street Bridge into Alexandria, Virginia. 45 minutes later, Phatmama pulled in the horseshoe driveway behind Rocco's Benz truck.

Adjusting his dick in his pants, Rocco got out of his whip and gave up the coolest walk a nigga could give from DC. "You ready?" Rocco asked, looking strangely at Phatmama. "Damn, you got them big-ass Gucci shades on and that big-ass hat on like you creeping out on your man or something?" Rocco stated.

"Rocco don't be hating because my shit is on fleek!" Phatmama said, laughing. "Grab my bag out the back, and I'm ready." Phatmama hit the release button on her key remote and the Navigator hatch lifted in the air.

Rocco walked to the back of the truck and his eyes popped out when he was greeted by a masked man holding a chrome .44. He tried to reach for the Berretta he had on his hip, but the cold steel of Phatmama's 9mm strongly encouraged him not to do anything stupid. "Fuck," he mumbled, clenching his jaws together.

The masked man relieved Rocco of the gun he had concealed on his hip. "Let's go!" Phatmama ordered.

Rocco took his walk of shame to the front door of his house and unlocked the front door. He couldn't believe he let a bitch trick him like that, and a chubby bitch at that. If he made it up out of this, Cain was going to chew his ass out about it.

"Hold up! When we get in here, deactivate the alarm. If you put some bullshit in the game, I'm going to put hot shit in your brain," the masked man stated.

Hearing the voice of the person behind the mask let Rocco know the person who was clutching the big-ass revolver was not a man at all, but a woman, which in turn made him madder. Rocco shook his head and did what he was told. He deactivated the alarm, walking in.

The 6,500 square-foot Colonel-style home on the outskirts of Alexandria was immaculate. The five bedroom and three-and-a-half bathroom house was the dream home for many women. The kitchen was flawless and complimented the black-and-gray Italian tile on the floor, set perfectly with the cream-colored Swedish leather sectional sofa and recliners. Everything about the house reflected money.

"Damn!" the masked woman said, stepping into the house behind Phatmama. What really caught her attention was the diamond chandelier hanging from the ceiling. She had to chuckle at the life-size picture on the wall of Rocco. Rocco was shirtless, flexing his abs while brandishing a Draco with a hundred-round drum connected to it. The picture even had a title to it. It read: *BOSS OF BOSSES*. Some niggas be doing way too much, and Rocco was one of them.

"Strip ass-naked and get yo' bitch-ass on the floor," Phatmama ordered.

"Bitch, I'm not getting naked. If you came here for the bread, then take it and get the fuck on," Rocco retorted.

Phatmama placed the gun beside Rocco's ear and pulled the trigger. *Boom!* The gun barked, sending Rocco's ears ringing.

"Argh!" He fell to the floor, grabbing ahold of his ears.

Phatmama watched him as he squirmed and hollered like a bitch. "Get the fuck up! And get naked like I told your bitch-ass," Phatmama screamed.

Rocco struggled to his feet, still holding his ear. He could feel the blood running from his ear from his eardrum rupturing. Rocco came into compliance, kicking off his Gucci loafers, and his whole Gucci attire came behind them. The tile was cool on Rocco's skin.

"Billie, tie his ass up," Phatmama instructed.

Billie did her job like an expert. She first tied Rocco's hands behind his back, then rolled him over and tied his ankles and knees together. The way Billie tied him up confirmed to Rocco that she had done this many times before. He wasn't going to get free from her bonds, no matter what.

Phatmama dropped a black bag beside Rocco's head. The bag's contents clicked and clanked together as the bag hit the floor. "Okay, Rocco. Let's play a game. It's called 'I ask and you tell,'" Phatmama stated, squatting down over top of Rocco's head and tracing her 9mm around the outline of his face. "Where the money at?"

Rocco swallowed hard. He was hesitant to tell Phatmama where the money was, but the thumping feeling in his right ear encouraged his decision. "It's upstairs in the master bedroom, under the bed."

"Naw, Rocco, that's that sucka money. That's that money you give one of them amateurs that never rob nothing. You give them that small money, hoping they leave, but the whole time you got the big stash hid somewhere else. I want the big stash, Rocco. Where that shit at?"

"Bitch, I ain't giving your fat ass shit!" Rocco screamed.

"Ok, have it your way," Phatmama calmly said, opening the duffle bag and setting a bundle of coat hanger wire on the floor. Then she removed a mini blowtorch, along with some welding gloves. Last, but not least, Phatmama pulled a bottle of Johnson & Johnson baby oil out of the bag.

Seeing the equipment Phatmama placed on the floor made Rocco's mouth become dry. He peeked over at the masked robber, who he had heard Phatmama call Billie. He could see she bared a smile on her face that gave her dark gray eyes behind the mask a look of sadness.

"I'm going to have some fuckin' fun with your tough ass,"

Phatmama said, now sharing a smile of her own. "Billie, do you want to do the honors?"

"I most definitely would. I don't plan on getting much blood on my hands tonight." Billie took the mask off her head for the first time. Her short, bleached white hair blended perfectly with her enchanting eyes.

Billie bit down on her bottom lip as she eyed Rocco's manhood. "Chocolate!" she exclaimed, grabbing the bottle of baby oil. She poured a good amount over Rocco's limp penis. "Damn, honey, all this chocolate," Billie said in her Southern voice. She grabbed Rocco's dick and let the slickness of the baby oil bring him to life as she worked her hand up and down.

Rocco tried his best not to let his oppressor's hand job arouse him, but little Rocco had a mind of his own.

"Come on, big daddy. Give mama this hunk of chocolate," Billie said, still feverishly working Rocco's rod in her had. She could feel him grow in the palm of her hand.

Getting him bricked like she wanted him, Billie slapped Rocco's dick against her face and lips a few times She couldn't resist the chance to feel Rocco's dick on her face. She grab him by the base of his chocolate manhood and squeezed him tightly, making the mushroom head swell. "Get 'im!" Billie yelled out.

Phatmama grabbed a coat hanger rod, oiled it down, and inserted it in the opening of Rocco's dick. "Argh!" Rocco cried out.

"Shut the fuck up! You haven't felt any pain yet," Phatmama stated.

Rocco could feel the coat hanger being pushed down into his shaft, all the way down to his bladder. "Please, don't do this," Rocco squirmed and pleaded.

"Nah, I asked you a simple-ass question, and you answered with calling me a bitch." Phatmama placed the welder's glove on her hand and picked up the blowtorch, putting a spark to it.

The blowtorch blew fearsomely with a roar. Phatmama grabbed ahold of Rocco's manhood with her gloved hand. She took the blowtorch and let the flame itch roll over the coat hanger that was hanging six inches out of his penis. Instantly the rod turned red hot and severe heat traveled down into Rocco's manhood.

"Argh! Argh!" Rocco screamed like a mad man. The room lit up with the smell of burning flesh. Phatmama kept running the torch over the rod. Rocco bucked hard, but still Phatmama refused to let go of his dick.

"What the fuck is that smell?" Billie said, scrunching up her face and putting a hand over her nose.

A brown puddle started to form under Rocco. His bowels released, souring the tile floor he lay on. Rocco never experienced pain like he was feeling. He'd been shot two times before, but that pain couldn't come close to what he was feeling at the moment.

Phatmama finally released Rocco and watched in amazement as he squirmed and wiggled with his hands behind his back.

"Argh! Argh! Argh!" Rocco moaned in pain through clenched teeth.

"Now, I'm going to ask you again where is that stash?" Phatmama asked, turning the fire up on the torch.

This time Rocco didn't waste time conveying the information Phatmama requested. "It's be–. It's behind the-the portrait on the wall." Beads of sweat had accumulated on Rocco's forehead and his naked chest.

Billie walked over to the life-size portrait of Rocco holding his gun and flexing his stomach muscles. She removed the picture to find a large safe resting behind it. "What's the combo?" Billie asked.

"10-4-79," Rocco mumbled and prayed he would make it out of this situation alive.

"Da-yam, Mr. Chocolate! It's loaded." Billie stared at the money stacked high and deep in the safe.

"Load it up, Billie, so we can get the fuck up outta here," Phatmama said, turning her blowtorch up even higher. "You know why I'm doing this?" Phatmama asked, stooping down over Rocco.

Her captive couldn't speak. He was too busy praying.

"I'm doing this because niggas like you be doing the most. You use the money you have to demoralize the women you come in contact with. You treat them like shit. You step on them, abuse them just because they are women. But the revelation is men like you are really the women because you are the true bitches."

Phatmama placed the flame of her blowtorch on Rocco's nut sack. The extreme heat made his nuts blister.

"Argh! Shit! Please, stop," Rocco begged for mercy.

"I got it all," Billie called out with two duffle bags over her shoulders and holding her .44 in her hand.

"Damn. I would have loved to finish torturing his ass," Phatmama said, pointing her gun to Rocco's head and pulling the trigger.

Boom! It knocked his brains onto the tile floor. The mess looked like someone spilled a bowl of Spaghetti-O's.

Phatmama bent back down and continued to work Rocco's nuts and dick over with the blowtorch until it was nothing but a black, charred mess.

Billie watched Phatmama work, shaking her head side-to-side. "You are one sick mama, melting down all that good chocolate like that. Chocolate suppose melt in your mouth, and not in your hands."

"Girl, hush! You didn't want that chocolate, anyway. That chocolate didn't have any sugar in it. That's that diabetic chocolate," Phatmama said, laughing, put her tools away, and went to retrieve the bag of money Rocco informed them was under his bed.

Phatmama felt good as her and Billie made their way out the door with Rocco's money. Billie slid her mask back on as she walked out behind Phatmama.

Chapter 11

Jelli opened her eyes and smiled at the soreness she was feeling in between her legs. Last night's back breaking lovemaking rendezvous with Cain was on a level she never encountered in her 26 years of living. The crisp Burberry sheets felt amazing under her skin. The sheets held the scent of their lovemaking and a hint of Cain's Tom Ford fragrance. Jelli inhaled deeply, trying to savor the two scents, which smelled exotic entwined together.

Jelli and Cain had been seeing each other for the past nine months. They had met by fate when Cain accidentally bumped into Jelli, knocking her iPhone 6 out of her hand and shattering the screen when the phone hit the floor.

"Damn, my bad, baby girl," Cain said, watching the phone break into pieces. He tried to catch the phone before it hit the ground, but he wasn't successful.

Jelli's face turned into a mask of ugliness. "Damn, your bad? That's it? What about my damn phone?" Jelli stated, picking her broken phone up off the mall floor.

Cain had a good chance to really look at Jelli, and his mind was blown by her beauty. Her toned thighs flexing against her Seven jeans made it seem as if the material was painted on her. A little voice in the back of his head told him he had to have her.

"Don't trip, I gotcha," Cain said, grabbing Jelli by the hand and leading her to the T-Mobile store, which was only two stores down from the Victoria's Secret shop. Cain took Jelli to the counter. "Um, excuse me, can I please have the newest iPhone 7?" Cain said, sending the clerk to retrieve the phone.

"What? You going to buy me a new phone?" Jelli asked in disbelief.

"Yeah, I broke the old one, right?" Cain shot back with a

smile.

For the first time, Jelli took in Cain's appearance and features. He towered over her with his 6'2" frame. His chestnut eyes went perfectly with his brown-skinned complexion, and he had a killa smile. Examining his Tom Ford attire from his shoes to his shirt, she knew he was a man who took pride in the way he dressed. And everything about him demonstrated money, especially the diamond-embedded AMP bigheaded watch he rocked like it was an everyday G-shock. Jelli knew the watch was worth at least 400 bands, easily.

They exchanged names and numbers. Cain's charm was a breath of fresh air to Jelli, and he had no problem convincing her to accompany him to Moe's Crab House for some lunch. The duo hit it off instantly, and ever since that day the two had been spending many nights together. But Jelli wasn't ready to introduce Cain to her girls due to the fact he wasn't too forthcoming about how he was getting his money, and Jelli wasn't ready to reveal how she was obtaining hers, either. Plus, on top of that, Jelli didn't want to hear Rico's mouth about bringing Cain around.

Jelli rolled over and saw the clock next to the bed read 8:15 a.m. She stretched her body and reached over to where Cain should have been, but he wasn't there. Jelli wondered where he could be.

She got out of the California King bed and stepped into her purple boy shorts that lay on the floor next to the bed. She pulled a button-down Polo shirt over her head bare-breasted and went to find her man.

Jelli loved the five-bedroom, three-bath home with a built-in theater, a huge kitchen with a cooking island in the middle, and a grill. Everything was black and stainless steel. The marble floor was cool under her bare feet as her pretty toes pitter-pattered against the floor.

She knew where to find him, so she made her way to Cain's office. She eased up to the door so she could hear him talking.

"Do you know who could have done this?"

Cain gave a pause to let whoever he was talking to have a chance to reply to his question. Jelli paused at the door.

"What about the work?" Cain questioned.

Jelli stood at the door, not sure if she should walk in or leave, but she was like any other girl from the hood – she was nosy as hell.

"Okay, get the security footage and bring it to me. Before you leave, call the police on the burner phone, and make sure you don't touch shit. The streets gonna bleed for this shit here," Cain said, pushing the end button on his phone and dropping his phone on his office desk.

In frustration, Cain placed his face in the palms of his hands and rested his elbows on the desktop. Thoughts ran through his mind of who wanted to kill his cousin. Tears started to well up in his eyes. He couldn't believe his cousin was gone, and he died under his watch while working for his organization. Tears cascaded down this cheeks.

Jelli stood in the doorway watching Cain. She could feel his pain from where she stood. She didn't want to do nothing but help her man through whatever he was going through. She had heard Cain's whole conversation, and her being a bitch from the streets, she easily filled in all the blanks.

Jelli approached Cain in his grieving state and placed a hand on his shoulder. Cain jumped from Jelli's sudden presence. He immediately wiped the tears away with his right hand. He tried to speak, but Jelli silenced him by covering his lips with her hand.

"Let me take care of you, baby. Let me heal you," Jelli said, lowering herself between Cain's legs and releasing his limp member from his sweatpants.

"Jelli, you–"

"Shh!" Jelli hushed Cain. She softly licked the head of his love stick, and in the blink of an eye the soft and warm wetness of her mouth brought Cain's dick to life. "Let me take your pain away, Cain," Jelli whispered, placing him in the back of her throat.

Cain closed his eyes and did just that.

***

Justin Greene sat in the back of the 2017 GMC, shaking in fear. Sweat dotted his forehead as he sat as still as he possibly could. The bomb vest that was strapped to his chest seemed like it was twenty pounds and gave him the eerie feeling it would explode at any given moment.

"You ready for this?" the Muslim lady asked in her full Islamic garments. She held a black .45 in her hand, and it was pointed dead between the eyes of Justin.

"Y-Yeah. I'm ready," he stuttered.

"Before you go in, take a look at your family one last time, in case you go in there and do some shit you ain't supposed to do," the Muslim lady said. She handed him an iPad.

The image of his beautiful wife and precious daughters was displayed on the screen with another Muslim woman, covered from head to toe, holding his family at gunpoint. Justin swallowed hard. He stared at the faces of his wife and kids. He saw nothing but straight terror in their expressions.

Justin was a man of habit. Every morning he ate breakfast with his wife and kids and headed to work while drinking his morning coffee, but this morning was different for him. He was met by three Muslim women as he came out of his Adams Morgan home. They forced him inside at gunpoint and took his family hostage. Their demands were for him to go into the check-cashing place where he worked and empty out the safe and deposit boxes or his family would die a terrible death. Justin knew these people were professionals as well as savages when he seen how skillfully one of them cut the thumb off his wife's hand just to give him more motivation to complete the task at hand.

The robbers knew everything about him, including him being the manager at the check-cashing place. Justin couldn't let his family die, so he agreed to the robbers' terms.

"Yeah, I'm ready," he stated, taking a deep breath and wiping sweat from his eyes.

"Alright, y'all, let's do it. The money train has left the station," the Muslim woman said into her Bluetooth earpiece.

"All eyes on the train," a voice came back through the earpiece.

The Muslim woman looked at Justin through her veil. Justin couldn't see her eyes, but she could see his, and they held nothing but revulsion in them.

"Alright, Justin, move your ass. You got four minutes to walk out the check-cashing place with this bag full of money. And remember two things while you in there. One, your family's lives are at stake, and if you not out in four minutes, I'm going to hit this button and *boom*! Your ass is no longer in existence," the Muslim lady said, pointing to the bomb detonator she held in her gloved hand.

Justin didn't talk. He just pulled the suit jacket over the boom vest and exited the GMC truck, walking briskly across 14th Street with a black bag in his hand. The check-cashing place sat in the middle of 14th and Spring Road and Park Place. Justin entered his workplace just like any other morning. Reaching the secured door that separated the customers from the employers, Justin waited for Sandy to buzz him in. The door's security locks clicked, allowing him access behind the glass counters.

"Good morning!" Sandy said to her boss. Justin brushed her off and headed straight to the safe to relieve it of its small and large bills. He then glanced at his Timex watch and seen two minutes had passed already. He rushed to the cash drop box and punched in his code. The doors opened instantly. Justin started dumping it contents in the black bag he carried.

Sandy watched in confusion. "Mr. Greene, what are you doing?" Sandy questioned her boss.

Her panicked tone alerted the other staff members, who watched Mr. Greene dump the money into the bag.

Justin ignored her, zipped the bag, and made his way to the security door to be let back out to the other side of the counter. "Sandy, buzz me out."

"Hell naw, I'm not going to let you walk out of here with that money. You robbing this place, Mr. Greene! I'm calling the police," Sandy announced.

"Bitch, open the fucking door!" he yelled, opening his suit jacket, displaying the bomb strapped to his chest.

Jelissa, another employee, fainted upon seeing the bomb harnessed to Justin's chest. Sandy took two long seconds as she was hitting the security button, releasing the latch that secured the door. Hearing the door click, Justin stepped through it with purpose.

Sandy hit the silent alarm.

In seconds, Justin was at the truck handing the Islamic-looking woman the bag. "You got your money, now let my family go," Justin pleaded.

"I always keep my word," the Muslim woman said. "Before I go, when the police get here, tell them The Red Bottom Bitches struck again," she said from the passenger side of the truck as the driver pulled away from the curb, leaving Justin standing there, dumbfounded.

***

"Damn, we did it!" Tata screamed once her, Jelli, and Zoey got to the location where they ditched the stolen truck. Zoey drove a black Honda. She sat four cars down from Tata and Jelli, across the street from the check-cashing place. Her job was to open fire on anything that looked like it was going to come between them and the money. They changed clothes, and Jelli got behind the waiting wheel of the Ford Fusion rental. Tata jumped in the passenger seat and Zoey hopped in the back seat and laid her Mini-14 across her lap. They made a right on Georgia Avenue.

Tata opened the bag that sat between her green-colored Red Bottoms. Stacks of cash stared back at her. She smiled and closed the bag back.

DC metropolitan police cars shot by them, heading toward the unfortunate check cashing place. Jelli played her mirrors as her hand rested on her pink Glock that was tucked between her legs.

"That bitch Phatmama is a straight beast for putting this shit together," Zoey stated from the back seat. "I mean, we robbed that spot without even having to step foot in that bitch."

"Like what Arianna said: That's what bad bitches do," Tata said, giving Jelli a high five.

"Shit, all we got to do now is get the merchandise sold from the Zales heist and we good," Jelli said, not letting Tata forget she still had a task to complete.

"I'm still working on that as we speak." But the truth was Tata really wasn't sure how she was going to swap the jewelry for cash.

Catching the red light at Georgia and Park Road, the trio played the mirrors on the rental. Action at the gas station on their right caught the attention of Tata. Three masked men came running out of the Amoco.

The owner of the establishment came running out behind them. *Ka-Boom*! The shotgun roared in the owner's hand.

The robber with the red bandanna on his face spun around and released two shot from a hand cannon. *Boom! Boom!*

The gas station owner flinched and took some cover as he felt two bullets whiz past his head. But that didn't take the fight out of him. He cocked the slide-back on the 12-gauge to chamber another double-R slug. He took aim. *Ka-Boom*! The 12-gauge kicked hard in his hand, sending a slug out of the barrel, which found a home in the back of one of the robbers. The impact of the slug knocked the robber forward, sending him sailing into the air and slamming him to the pavement.

Boom! Boom! The robber with the red bandanna's gun roared again, striking the owner in the shoulder with a hollow-point, making him spin around and lose the shotgun in the process.

The first robber made it to the getaway car, not giving the robber in the red bandanna a chance to get in the car before he pulled away from the curb, leaving his partner behind.

Tata, Zoey, and Jelli watched in amazement. Tata noticed something about the remaining robber: he had titties.

A police car slid into the gas station. The first responder was riding solo. The robber didn't give the officer time to place the police cruiser in park before she sent a bullet through the windshield and planting it in the officer's chest.

Boom! The bullet from the cannon rocked the officer forward, misting blood all over the windshield.

The robber could hear sirens echoing in the distance. She knew more police were on their way, and it wasn't smart for her to stick around. She took off in a sprint while reloading her gun at the same time.

"Damn, you see that shit?" Jelli said with excitement in her voice.

"Yeah, we got to help her! Go follow her," Tata yelled.

"Bitch, are you fucking crazy?" Jelli said, looking at Tata like she done lost her mind.

"Jelli, just go! You wasting time," Tata ordered.

Jelli gritted her teeth and floored the Fusion, bending the corner where she seen the robber flee. Tata was sitting up in her seat, trying to find the robber and spotting her at the end of the block. Tata seen her pull the black Washington Nationals cap off her head and pull the red bandanna away from her face.

Jelli pulled up beside her. Tata yelled from the passenger window, "Aye, get in."

The sudden appearances of the car and Tata yelling startled the robber, which made her draw the .357 from her hip and aim it at Tata.

The Mini-14 came from the back window. "Bitch, I wish you would," Zoey said, pointing the assault rifle at the hostile robber.

"Do you want to go to jail, or you want to get away? Get the fuck in the car," Tata yelled.

The robber eyed Tata and Zoey, then shrugged her shoulders, tucked her gun on her hip, and jumped in the back seat with Zoey and laid across the floor of the car.

As soon as Jelli was turning off the block, a cop car was bending the corner.

Jibril Williams

Chapter 12

"This scaredy-ass nigga left me for dead. I swear on blood, I'm murkin' that ass the first chance I get, homie," Racks said, pacing back and forth across the dingy carpet of the Budget Inn floor. "I appreciate everything you all did for me," Racks said, stopping and staring into the eyes of her three rescuers.

"That shit ain't about nothing. We seen you in distress and thought you could use a hand," Tata retorted, placing some fire to the end of the freshly-twisted blunt.

Jelli rolled her eyes. "No, you wanted to help her," Jelli stated with irritation in her voice, letting Tata know she wasn't happy about helping the outsider.

Racks stared at Jelli with her face knotted up. Her hand dropped down to her waist, where her black Python .357 rested. "Baby, are we cool or what? Because I didn't ask you to stick your neck out for me," Racks questioned.

Jelli seen Racks' hand movement, and it put her on defense. "Bitch, I ain't ducking no rec." Jelli jumped up, knocking the hotel chair over in the process, and reached for her Glock.

"Jelli!" Tata yelled. "Pipe the fuck down!"

Jelli and Racks stared at each other with a savage look in their eyes as their hands rested on the handles of their weapons. Jelli was the first to break eye contact. "Whatever, Tata!" Jelli stated and walked out of the room, slamming the door behind her.

Zoey watched Racks with her own hand on her gun. Even though she was infatuated with Racks' swag, she wouldn't hesitate to knock her noodles loose. Her loyalty was definitely with Jelli. Zoey found Racks' tatted arms interesting. She knew the tats told a story of who Racks really was, and she wanted to read every page of her.

The way Racks rocked her two braids and the body ink

made her strongly resemble the rapper M.I.A. Racks carried her 157 pounds with great ease. It fit well on her 5'7" frame. Her walnut-brown eyes held pain, pleasure, murder, and love in them.

Zoey didn't know why the crotch of her panties was soaked. Even though she'd had the honor of experiencing a woman eating her inside out, she still preferred dick over pussy any day. But being in the presence of this thugged-out woman created a desire in her that wanted to see what Racks was all about.

"Listen, Racks, we got to make moves, so we gonna bounce. But if you really trying to secure that bag, then hit me up," Tata said, picking Racks' phone up off the table and programming her number into it. "Hit me up so we can link up. And stay the fuck out them gas stations. Them bitches don't have no money in them, so there's no benefit in robbing them."

Racks wasn't really feeling how Tata was talking to her. Everyone had a way of getting their own cash, so she didn't know why Tata was knocking hers. "Yeah, I hear ya," Racks replied. Tata passed her the burning blunt. "Once again, I appreciate the assistance you gave a gangsta. Hopefully I can one day repay the favor," Racks said, accepting the blunt and taking a long pull off it.

"Well, you can repay me by just hitting me up when you get a chance, and let's talk."

Racks was curious why Tata had helped her and wanted her to link up with her. And why were Tata and her girls riding around in a Ford with all the firepower? But she didn't pry. Her main focus was to find out how bad that police officer was hurt and if they had any leads on the shooter. Plus, she needed some alone time to think and reach out to her big homie, Whip. "I'll check you when shit die down with me. Right now I'm just trying to touch bases with my blood family," Racks said.

"I can understand that. So, with that being said, we out,"

Tata said, exiting the room.

Zoey took a few seconds to look Racks over one last time. She twirled the grape Blow Pop on her tongue and popped the sucker out of her mouth, making a popping sound, and rolled her tongue over her lips and walked out behind Tata, closing the door behind her and leaving Racks gripping the crotch of her black Billionaire jeans like she really had a dick.

***

Jelli sat in the rental, fuming mad. She was hotter than Wings & Things' deep fryers. She'd just gotten off the phone with Phatmama, explaining to her the crazy shit Tata had pulled. Phatmama wanted to come grab the money from them that they just robbed the check cashing place for, but Jelli didn't want to bring too much attention to them, so she assured Phatmama they would be there soon.

Jelli watched Tata and Zoey exit the hotel room. She started the car. Tata and Zoey climbed in.

"Tata, what the fuck was that shit you pulled?" Jelli questioned. Before Tata could answer, she went into vent mode. "You broke protocol and exposed your team to unnecessary danger," Jelli stated through clenched teeth, eyeing Tata like she was crazy.

Tata let out a deep breath. "Look, *mami*, you right. I put the team in danger, and for that you all can break my cut of the money down with the team if you feel that would make everyone happy. But put yourself in Racks' shoes. She was in a fuck position and she needed help."

"Tata, fuck that pussy-gobbling-ass bitch! She's not family."

Tata couldn't take it no longer. She had to check Jelli, she was the leader of this clique, and she demanded respect and for a bitch not to question her every call. "Jelli, I'm going to say this shit once, and I'm not gonna tell your ass again. Honor the oath. If one ride, we all roll. If one hesitate, we all motivate. And if one betrays, know that God forgives. We don't," Tata stated calmly. "I remember a time on Hazelton Yard when your ass needed some much-needed help, and who came to rescue that ass?"

Immediately Jelli's mind flashed back to that prison yard. Six members of the G-27 gang surrounded Jelli by the handball court. Jelli was fairly new to the prison. The G-27 leader was looking to recruit new members to the gang or find a new candidate to ride their tongue after the midnight count. Jelli made the fatal mistake of accepting a care package from the G-27s, which consisted of hygiene items.

"Yo, Jelli, what's good, baby? I heard you turned down the offer to join our fine organization."

Jelli could feel the tension building up around her, but she was far from a bitch, so she was waiting for the right moment to make her move. "I done told your shot-caller that I respectfully decline her offer," Jelli said, eyeing the 265-pound giant of a woman who stood 6'2".

"So, you must be willing to lick and set that pussy out to the G-27s on demand like Netflix, because that care package you received didn't come cheap." Anna stated, stepping closer into Jelli's firing range.

Jelli wasted no time. She threw the haymaker and connected with Anna's jaw. The surprise, lightening-speed blow rocked Anna, bringing her down to her knees.

The other five gang members attacked Jelli relentlessly. Jelli got punched in the eye, which made her see nothing but stars, then the prison yard dirt that powdered her face as she slammed into the ground. All she could feel now were prison boots finding homes on her head, back, and stomach. All she could do was ball up in a fetal position and hope the C.O.s got there before the G-27s killed her.

All of a sudden the blows she was once receiving were now nonexistent. Jelli peeked from under her arms to see a group of girls fighting off her attackers. Jelli couldn't let them have all the fun. She jumped up and helped those who were helping her.

Those same people she became unconditionally loyal to. Those same people who helped her was sitting in the car with her.

"I understand where you are coming from." Jelli's demeanor softened a bit. "It's just that we can't trust these bitches out here in these streets," Jelli said, pulling the rental out of the Budget Inn parking lot into New York Avenue midday traffic.

"Yeah, you right, but sometimes out here in these streets you have to go with your gut instinct, and my instinct told me to help Racks. And the way that bitch handled that big-ass gun made me think we can use a bitch like that on our team."

"You ain't lyin'. Racks was like Jesse James out that bitch wit' that big-ass revolver," Zoey chimed in from the back seat.

Jelli rolled her eyes at Zoey through the rearview mirror. "Well, let's hope that shit don't come back and haunt us, because I wouldn't hesitate to smash that M.I.A.-looking bitch," Jelli said with venom in her voice.

"Did Phatmama call?" Tata asked, changing the subject.

"You know she did," Jelli said, making a left at the intersection of New York Avenue and Florida Avenue, heading toward Benning Road.

"Well, let's get to the house so we can count this money up," Tata said, tapping the bag that rested between her legs as her mind wondered if she made the right move by helping Racks.

Only time would tell.

Jibril Williams

Chapter 13

Two Hours Later

"Oh my fucking God! $157,000!" Zoey said, hypnotized by the money resting on the dining room table.

Seeing all the money gave Jelli the sense her life of crime was paying off, but to Tata this was brown paper bag money, and she didn't have a desire but to be a boss and make boss moves. A petty $157,000 wasn't nowhere near boss status in her eyes.

Phatmama wasn't even fazed by the money. She'd done seen plenty in the last year. She was more than happy with seeing her girls happy, though.

"So, that's 25 bands apiece," Tata said, pouring Hennessey Black into four shot glasses sitting next to the money on the table.

"Um, Tata, I don't know where you learned how to do math, but in my school 25 bands apiece times four equals to 100 bands. You forgot about the other 57 bands," Zoey stated, looking crazy at Tata.

"When I was in the streets in Miami, I was taught when you out here breaking law and bending corners, you put up lawyer and bail money, and that's what that other 57 bands is going toward. We gotta start thinking ahead and thinking as a unit. We got to think big. We can't keep doing this shit forever. We too damn fine to be going back to a federal prison. We got to start saving money to go legit."

All parties nodded their heads in agreement. Tata pushed each of her girls 25 stacks apiece with the shot of Hennessey. Tata held her shot glass in the air. Zoey, Phatmama, and Jelli did the same. "To black diamonds and Red Bottoms!"

The women repeated behind Tata, and they downed the dark

liquor. "Woo!" Zoey said through watery eyes. The Hennessey Black burned her throat as it went down.

"So, that's our handle now, huh?" Phatmama asked with a smirk on her face.

"Huh? Girl, what are you talking about?" Tata asked curiously.

"Black diamonds and Red Bottoms."

"Shit, bitch, you know that shit got a catch to it. That's what the media has dubbed us. The robbers who wore Red Bottoms doing a heist and made away with $360,000 worth of black diamonds," Tata said, shrugging her shoulders and pouring herself another shot of Hennessey.

"Are we ever going to be able to get off that jewelry for the Zales heist?" Jelli inquired.

"Well, I think we going to get rid of the jewelry, but the black diamonds is going to be a task to do so," Tata said, downing her second shot of Hennessey.

"Why is that?" Zoey chimed in.

"Well, the whole fucking world is looking and inquiring about where those diamonds are located. It wouldn't be in our best interest to try to move them diamonds at this time, but the other jewelry we can move," Tata said.

"When can we get off the goods? Do you have a buyer?" Jelli shot question after question at Tata while she broke down some high-grade bud inside a Backwood wrap.

"I'm still working on that. I was thinking about Rico's buyer."

"What? Tata, you are tripping? He will tell Rico, and how do you know you can trust him?" Phatmama asked.

"I don't, but I'm going to find out, though," Tata retorted, thumbing through her stack of money.

"Well, at least have you gotten a chance to meet him and got a feel for him?" Jelli asked, putting a finishing seal to the

Backwood with her tongue.

"I only met him once, but let me work on it. But in the meantime, spend this money slowly until we can put something else together," Tata instructed.

Jelli sparked the cherry on the Backwood, letting the weed invade her lungs. She closed her eyes and held the smoke captive in her lungs, then let the smoke out slowly and passed the Backwood to Tata.

"Damn, *mami*, the way you closed your eyes and shit was like you was letting the weed bring you to a orgasm," Tata joked.

"You can tell by how that shit smells that's some good shit. Hurry up and pass the Backwood, Tata," Phatmama pressed.

"You one of the Black and Decker-type of bitches, can't wait to suck a bitch's shit up," Tata shot at Phatmama. The women fell out in laughter.

"Girl, shut the fuck up and pass that shit," Phatmama said, reaching over the table and grabbing the bottle of Hennessey Black to refill her glass.

"See, Tone! I told you these bitches was up to no fucking good," Rico said, walking into the dining room and startling the women.

Tata fumbled the Backwood she held to her lips. It hit the floor, knocking the cherry from the tip of it. She promptly picked the Backwood up from the floor before it could burn a hole in the carpet. The women tried to shield and ease the money from the table, but their efforts were fruitless.

"Don't hide it, divide it," Rico said, grabbing the 57 bands resting on the middle of the table. "I see everyone got their issue, so I guess this me, right here?"

No one in the room spoke a word. Phatmama's blood began to boil.

Rico held the stacks of money under his nose and inhaled

deeply. "Damn, I love the smell of money. When I heard the police scanner go off reporting a robbery just took place and the suspects escaped in a dark-colored truck wearing Islamic clothing and Red Bottoms, I told my nigga Tone here," Rico said, pointing at his crime partner who stood in the doorway with a sly grin on his face, "that you bitches just robbed that check cashing place. So here we are, and behold, there's money in you all's presence that I'm sure you can't properly explain how you came upon this money," Rico said, smiling as if he was the smartest nigga in the world.

All eyes laid on Rico. Tata was frozen like a deer caught in the headlights.

"Hold up, Rico. You just can't come in here and take our money," Jelli spoke up.

"Bitch, is you fucking stupid?" Rico raised his voice. "You forgot who taught you how to clutch a Glock? You forgot who sent you all out to Utah for Handz to train you bitches, huh? I invested in you bitches, and trust me, I'm planning to get what I invested and more outta you all." Rico pause to see if anyone wasn't feeling what he was saying. "Or you bitches could turn over them black diamonds, and we can call it even."

Phatmama and Jelli made eye contact with Tata. Tata swallowed hard. "Rico, what black diamonds?" Tata said, trying to play dumb.

Rico looked at Tone and smirked, then turned his attention back to Tata. "The ones you came upon in the Zales heist."

"Psh! Rico, I told you that wasn't us," Tata stated, sucking her teeth and rolling her eyes.

Rico stared at Tata with rage in his eyes. He knew this bitch was straight-up lying, but he knew if he wanted to get his hands on them diamonds, he had to play his hand right. "I know you was all in on the heist and grabbed the diamonds. I also know you don't have a place to get off the merchandise. But if you need help wit' that, I'm your man," Rico said, pointing his index finger at himself.

Tata wasn't going for that shit he was trying to pull. She'd been lying in bed with this nigga long enough to know he was on some bullshit. "Rico, I'm telling you we didn't rob that Zales. Seeing how greedy you are for them diamonds and money, it's a good thing we didn't pull the heist," Tata said in disgust.

Rico shook his head from side to side. "I see you are ungrateful. I brought you into a life you never had. When I met you, you were begging for handouts on a prison pen pal site."

The words that flowed out of Rico's mouth hurt Tata deeply. The blow delivered in his words brought a greater pain than when she found out Rico had a baby on her. Tata's eyes misted over.

"I welcomed your dick-eating friends to my house when them bitches didn't have a place to live, gave them a place to wash their asses, shit, sleep, eat. And after all that you stank-ass bitches think you all don't owe me shit?" Rico screamed, spit sprayed from his mouth.

Phatmama hated that she left her gun in her truck. She would have blown Rico's brains out all over the wall. Rico's performance had placed him at the top of her kill list.

"Fuck you, Rico. You don't have to say all that shit," Jelli said with tears in her eyes. His words had stirred up some memories she wanted to forget about. "How much do we owe you? Because I don't want to be under your foot forever," Jelli asked, wiping tears from her face.

Rico looked at Jelli with malice. He knew he had them at his mercy. "Bitch, until I'm rich or you bitches die trying to make me rich," Rico stated, staring at the four women with a coldness in his eyes.

Right then and there, Tata seen something brewing in Rico's

eyes. She hadn't seen this look in a man's eyes since she was in the streets of Miami. The look she saw was murder.

"Now that we all on the same page, let me hear the rundown on the next lick. So get your panties out ya ass. We got money to make," Rico said, taking the Backwood out of Tata's hand and putting fresh fire to it.

Chapter 14

The small conference room was silent as the thick, white clouds danced in the air as gracefully as a ballerina. All eyes was on the 65-inch smart TV mounted to the wall before them. Sixteen pairs of eyeballs fought to identify the two women on the screen.

"Somebody knows something," Cain spoke calmly as he walked the room with hands behind his back. "Someone knows something. I mean, a muthafucka knows Rocco was my blood and under my umbrella of my organization and my protection. He gets murked and tortured, and no one knows shit?" Cain asked the group of men who occupied the room.

No one spoke a word. It was unwise to let Cain's calm demeanor fool them and put them in a trick bag. If anyone ever thought that D.C. infamous Wayne Perry was vicious, then Cain was three times worse.

"Ten blocks of pure heroin just disappeared, and no one knows a fuckin' thing?" Cain paced and stared in every man's eyes who occupied the room. His right-hand man, Fate, was also checking the eyes of the people in the room, hoping he could catch something in one of their eyes. It was known that the eyes told lies, and Fate was hoping to see it. "My patience is running thin. I want to know who those two bitches is," Cain stated, pointing at the smart TV screen.

The screen revealed a chunky-set woman wearing some big Gucci shades and a large hat. The other woman on the screen was impossible to identify due to her face being fully covered. The only reason they knew the masked person was a woman was because of the melon-sized breasts that could be see pressing against the fabric of her jacket. The security footage from Rocco's house also revealed the masked robber was white from the white skin that shown around the eye sockets of the mask she wore.

"Hold up. Back that shit up!" Cain called out.

Fate grabbed the remote and wound the footage back.

"Stop!" Cain said. The footage stopped on the back of the chunky woman's head. "Now zoom that shit in, slim," Cain instructed his partner. "Right there!" Cain said, pointing to the screen.

On the screen was the neck of the chunky woman. The image of a she-devil stared back at him. "If we find who bares this tattoo, we find out who killed my fucking cousin and who has my fucking work."

***

"Come on, nigga, stop playing with that shit. Break the fucking glass," Rico yelled through his mask while keeping his MP-5 trained on the hostages he had pinned down on the floor.

Diesel brought the mallet back over his head and brought it down on the glass display case with so much brute force that the vibrations from the contact almost made him lose the mallet. The glass of the display case remained intact. "Fuck!" Diesel screamed out.

Panic started to set in with Rico. They had been in McCormick & Smith's Jewelry for a full two minutes, and they hadn't started to fill their bag with the store valuables.

"Hop the counter!" Rico instructed, breaking protocol.

"What!" Diesel said from behind his mask.

"Nigga, you heard me! Hop the fucking counter! Four minutes!" Rico called out, starting the countdown over.

Diesel knew that was breaking all the rules in the jewelry heist game. One, never jump the counter. Some stores have silent alarms that can be triggered by stepping in a particular location on the floor behind the counter. And two, never restart a countdown.

Diesel hopped the counter where the store manager stood froze with his hands in the air. "Unlock the doors to the cases, cracker!" Diesel ordered the frightened store manager.

The Caucasian man's hands trembled hard like he had a bad case of Parkinson's disease when Diesel shoved the barrel of his 12-gauge sawed-off in the man's face.

"Move, bitch!" Diesel yelled.

The manager snapped out of his fear, suppressed his shakes, and started unlocking the glass display cases. Diesel was right behind him, trying to fill the bag he carried over his shoulder with jewelry. This process was slow, but Diesel was working as quickly as he could.

Tone hopped the counter to help empty out the display cases.

"Two minutes!" Rico informed his team.

Tone finished emptying out one of the display cases. He was moving to the next case and felt the floor slightly give. He knew he just triggered the silent alarm. The automatic magnetic locks on the door sounded off with a loud *Clack*!

Rico heard the locks click. "Fuck!" He could hear Tata in his earpiece informing him the call just came over the police scanner that a silent alarm was triggered at McCormick & Smith. "We gotta get outta here," Rico yelled, backing toward the door.

Tone and Diesel jumped back over the counter to where Rico was. Rico pulled on the door, but it was locked tight. He began to sweat under his mask. He wanted to remove the mask, but he fought to keep it on and hold his composure.

The thing about the magnet security-locking doors was they were designed to keep everyone in the store, but the flaw was they were designed to let the authorities in when they got there. All they had to do was touch the door handle on the outside of the door and the magnet locks would release so the police could gain access to the store.

Rico had broken all the protocols. He took his eyes off the hostages to take a shot at the door. *Rak-rak-rak-rak-rak-rak!* The MP5 thumped in Rico's hand, sending deadly bullets into the storefront glass.

The glass didn't shatter like it normally would. The bullets bounced off the glass. Seeing this drove him into straight panic mode. He let more shots off from his MP5. *Rak-rak-rak-rak-rak-rak-rak-rak-rak*! Rico still got the same results. "Fuck! Fuck!" Rico said, panicking and pulling on the door.

Rico saw a middle-aged white woman walking toward the door. She had her head down, preoccupied with her phone, texting away. She wasn't even paying attention to what was going on inside McCormick & Smith until she touched the door handle and hear the loud clicking of the magnetic lock, which made her look up from her phone.

The stock of Rico's shotgun landed on the bridge of her nose. "Let's go," Rico shouted.

One of the hostages on the floor made his move, everything was happening so fast it was a blur. "Freeze! F.B.–"

Boom! Tone's sawed-off pump chopped the hostage's words off.

The hostage barely cleared the .380 from his ankle holster before his chest was opened up from the impact of the 12-gauge. The opening in his chest looked like shredded meat. The hostage struggled to breathe, his ears ringing a bell only he could hear. Blood and tendons plastered the floor.

The store went into a frenzy. Diesel looked on in shock that Tone had the nuts to murk someone. Tone walked over and relieved the man of his gun that now laid next to his ankle.

An object was still gripped in the hostage's hand. Tone went for a closer look. He pulled back the hostage's fingers and a badge fell out with three letters stamped on it that every street nigga would hate to see. He stared down at the three letters, and the letters F.B.I. stared back at him.

"Aye, slim, this cracker a muthafuckin' fed."

Tone stood up, heading to the door in long strides. Rico and Diesel made it to the waiting car and waved Tone on. Tone stepped over the lady who lay in front of the door, holding her nose.

Tone broke out into a run and dove into the back seat of the stolen car. Diesel mashed the pedal to the metal and the car skidded away from the curb.

"Shit. Fuck!" Tone screamed out as he snatched his mask off his face. "I just killed a fucking fed."

No one spoke on the situation. All heads were on a swivel, on the lookout for any police.

Tone knew he had to get the fuck outta dodge ASAP! Shit was going to get heated real quick.

***

"Man, you need to hit Rau'f up tonight and holla at him ASAP. I need that bread," Tone said, pouring himself a drink with trembling hands. The liquor missed the glass and a little puddle formulated on the counter of the minibar. Tone had to concentrate hard to get his hand to stop shaking long enough to get the Ciroc in the shot glass. Filling the four-finger shot glass to the rim, he downed the liquid and refilled it.

"Slim, I'm not going to lie to you, it's going to be a minute before I can move the jewelry," Rico retorted, taking a pull from his Newport.

"Fuck that, Rico. I need you to work your mojo and get this shit moved," Tone said, nodding at the nine Cellini Rolex, five Anglesey, six Oyster Master watches and the slew of white gold, platinum, and gold jewelry discarded on the table. "I need that money to get the fuck out the city until shit cools down," Tone said, downing another shot.

"What the fuck you want me to do, Tone? Nobody in the United States is gonna touch this shit right now, 'specially when a dead fed is attached to this shit," Rico said with irritation in his voice, pointing at the merchandise that lay on the table.

"Well, I'm going to need a loan from you, then, until you can move this shit."

"Tone, I can't do that. I got my money tied in other shit right now."

"Well, untie that shit, because I got to get in the fucking wind." Tone placed his glass down on the mini bar and looked at Rico.

Tata wanted to shake her head so bad at Rico's pettiness. She knew without a doubt Rico had the money to put Tone on the road until shit calmed down.

"Man, I'm sorry, but my shit is tied up!" Rico took another drag of his Newport before smashing the butt out in the ashtray.

The muscle in Tone's jawline flexed. Rage was starting to build up in him as he seen what everything was hitting on. Rico was leaving him out to dry. The realization of this hit him like a ton of bricks. He was hazardous to Rico now, especially if the authorities ever found out he was behind the trigger that killed the F.B.I. agent. Shit had been on the news nonstop. Fox News found out through the deceased's parents that the off-duty agent went to the jewelry store to purchase an engagement ring for his girlfriend of three years. He was planning to propose to her that night at dinner.

"Slim, don't do this to me, Rico," Tone pleaded.

"I don't have the bread for you. What if the feds get on my line? I'm gonna need all the runes I got to escape them people, and we both know the feds are relentless."

"So, it's all about you after all the shit we been through?" Tone said, stepping behind the minibar, reaching for his strap.

Rico was a little quicker. He sprung to his feet in a quick motion and pulled his chrome fo'-fifth with the red diamond-encrusted handle. He pointed the gun at Tone. "Nigga, you trying me!" Rico said through clenched teeth.

"Hold the fuck up! You niggas tripping in this bitch!" Diesel said, coming up off the wall where he was watching all this shit unfold.

Tata remain seated with her legs tucked under her, watching with enthusiasm as if she was watching a clip from her favorite TV show, *Power*.

"What the fuck is wrong with you niggas? Shit go wrong and we fall apart and start pulling guns on each other? Come on, Rico, put the heat away," Diesel pleaded, inching toward Rico.

"Tell that nigga to fall the fuck back!"

Tone stared at Rico, unfazed at him pointing the gun at him, but he knew he was in a no-win situation, so he stepped from behind the bar, picked his shot glass back up, and took a sip of Ciroc. Tone never broke eye contact with Rico.

Diesel took a breath of relief seeing Tone come back in front of the minibar empty handed. Rico still had his gun in his hand. "Come on, Rico. He fell back, slim," Diesel stated, putting the palm of his hand in the middle of Rico's chest.

Rico listened to the youngster and lowered his weapon, but still gripped it firmly at his side.

Diesel could feel the rise and fall of Rico's chest. He knew Rico was heated, but he wanted to get the two apart before Rico or Tone did something stupid. "Listen, Tone," Diesel said, turning to face Tone. "I'm going to give you 30 bands, and when Rico unload the jewelry, I'll make sure you get your cut of the money."

"Naw, fuck that. I don't trust this nigga to play fair when

it's time for him to trade the jewels for cash. I'll take my cut right now in jewelry," Tone stated.

"Fuck, you crazy! Slim, you gonna go out there and try to sell this shit to a pawn shop or some corner nigga, and that shit gonna leave a trail, and all that's gonna do is make the feds box you in and tie you to the heist and that fed's murder."

"Nigga, you not the only one with connections! Give me mines," Tone demanded.

"You know, if your ass would have put up for a rainy day, then you wouldn't be here. Your ass would be hitting I-95, heading toward Miami or some-fucking-where." Rico knew he was going against his better judgment, but hell, he'd been doing that all day. He reluctantly pushed a few Rolexes, Cartier watches, diamond bracelets and rings to the side as he raked the rest of the jewelry back into the black bag. "This the end of us," Rico stated, handing Diesel the bag. "Tata, go start the car."

Rico toss her the keys to his 600. Tata caught the keys in midair, hopped to her feet, and made her way out of the house, hoping this situation with Rico and Tone wouldn't spill over on her if Tone decided to roll over on Rico for the way he handled him. Tata felt it would be a domino effect.

Tone took a sip from the liquor bottle. He'd graduated from the shot glass. "Nigga, I wouldn't have it no other way. I don't know why I even teamed up with a bamma-ass nigga like you." Tone's words came out of his mouth with venom in them.

Rico just stared at Tone with a smirk on his face he tapped the fo'-fifth against his leg. "I might be a bamma, but I'm not a broke bamma."

"Nigga, fuck you!" Tone mumbled. In his mind, Rico just slid the noose over his own neck. "Diesel, when can I get that scrilla?"

"I'll have that to you in about an hour. Just pack an' be ready to get the fuck outta here when I get back."

"Good. I'll be here when you get back. Don't leave me hanging. I'm depending on you, Diesel."

"Man, I gotcha. Just pack. I'll be back in an hour," Diesel said, walking out the door.

Rico backed out the door with a devilish grin on his face.

"There's an' old saying: what makes you smile will make you cry in the long run," Tone informed Rico.

Rico wanted badly to end Tone's life, but he knew the neighbors would surely hear the shots due to the houses being built so close together. Rico couldn't afford to take a chance, so he did what he had to, and that was save his bullets for Tone for another day when it would be more beneficial for him. "I wish shit didn't have to be this way," Rico said, backing out of the door and closing it."

"Yeah, me too, bitch-nigga," Tone said to himself, grabbing a latex glove from behind the minibar. He slid his hand inside the glove. Tone selected two pieces of jewelry off the table and placed them in a plastic bag. "I told you, nigga. What makes you laugh will make you cry."

Jibril Williams

Chapter 15

Phatmama, Zoey, and Jelli stayed up all night watching the news coverage on the murder of the off-duty F.B.I. agent. As of now, they didn't have any leads or suspects, but that could change real quick when fucking with the F.B.I., so that info brought only a small amount of relief to the trio. They knew with one of the F.B.I.'s very own being killed, they was going to use all their resources to bring whoever did this to justice.

"This shit is fucked up, Phatmama," Zoey said from the comfort of her loveseat.

Jelli blew out a cloud of smoke through her nose. She was in a daze. The Backwood burned slow between her fingers. She was wondering how shit went so wrong, and why didn't Rico exit the store once they couldn't crack the display case? "Greed is a muthafucka," Jelli mumbled to herself.

"Bitch, you ain't got to tell me, especially with Rico being the fucking crab he is and turnin' his back on Tone. If Tone get tagged for the F.B.I. murder, there's no doubt Tone wouldn't hesitate to give Rico and us up to the Feds," Phatmama said, wringing her hands together in frustration.

Tata had called late last night and told her everything that went down between Tone and Rico. Phatmama was thinking if she could get rid of the ten bricks she got off Rocco and the seven bricks she got off Bless, her and the girls could use that money to get out of dodge and away from Rico and just lay low. The hardest part about this was she didn't have a buyer for the drugs.

"You think if Rico or Tone got bagged for the murder, do you think they would keep it G and leave us out of the picture?" Jelli asked, breaking her silence.

"Shit, I don't know," said Phatmama, being quite honest.

"To be honest, Jelli, you know as well as I know, like Nikki

Tee said. 'these niggas ain't loyal,'" Zoey spoke, unwrapping a sour apple Blow Pop and placing it in her mouth

"The best thing for us to do is kill all them niggas so we don't have to worry about this shit coming back on us, or even worse, we take the fall for this shit," Jelli said, wiping the extra spit out of the corner of her mouth and looking at Phatmama and Zoey to see what type of feedback they was going to give her.

Phatmama looked at Jelli stone-faced, taking in everything she just said. Phatmama was unsure about Jelli when it came to Jelli taking a life. Truth be told, Jelli was the only person in the room that didn't have a murder under her belt. "Jelli, you my fucking girl and all, but murking a muthafucka isn't easy when you don't have it in you. Because once that body drop, ain't no coming back, baby." Phatmama was trying to lace Jelli with some game and see how she would respond.

"Fuck that. I'd rather murder a hundred niggas before I rot in a fucking prison cell," Jelli replied.

"Hold up, you all. What we gonna do about Tata?" Zoey inquired. "I mean, this is her man. The one she claims to love."

"If you thinking like that, you really don't know Tata. Tata is more loyal to us than Rico, and she ain't going to be that ride-or-die bitch for Rico because she knows Rico won't do it for her. And he already proved that a hundred times over," Phatmama spoke.

"Well, we need to do something about the problem while we got a chance," Jelli stated, taking another pull on the Backwood.

"You right," Phatmama agreed, pulling her phone out and sending Tata a text.

***

"Come on, Tone. Just take the money and bounce," Ace

whined cowardly. He lay tied up on the floor, watching Tone beat the fuck out of his twin brother, Deuce, with the handle of his .44. Blood oozed from all types of gashes the gun left on Deuce's head and face.

"Bitch-ass nigga! I leave when the fuck I'm ready, ho-ass nigga," Tone said with his arm midair. He was in the process of bringing the gun down on Deuce's face again.

Ace and Deuce were brothers Tone used to fuck with back in the day. The hustling game was too slow for Tone back then, so he chose to be a savage and get his the ski mask way. Tone and the brothers stayed in contact with one another, and when the twins ran into competition, Ace and Deuce would sic Tone on their competitors to rob them.

Tone stared down at Deuce's motionless body. The movement of his chest going up and down gave Tone the reassurance he was still alive. Standing up, Tone grabbed the book bag that contained the money he just hit the twins for.

Ace felt a sense of relief seeing Tone stand up and throw the bag strap over his shoulder. For a split second he thought he was going to make it out of the situation with his life. Until Tone stood over him and pointed the ugly-looking .44 at him. "Come on, man! Don't do this shit to me. You got the money, slim. You don't have to kill me," Ace begged and pleaded for his life.

Tone didn't want to kill the brothers or rob them, but whenever drastic times come into play, drastic measures were sure to follow. Killing a fed and being low on money had Tone standing overtop of Ace with a gun. The 30 bands Diesel gave him wasn't enough.

Tone took a deep breath and squeezed the trigger.
Boom! Boom!

The .44 Mag pushed Ace's head inward, pushing his brain out the other side of his head. His head burst open like a pumpkin that had been dropped from a second floor window. Blood and brain matter splattered on the floor.

Tone delivered Deuce the same fate as his brother, knocking a chunk of his face off. Tone walked out of the twins' crib with 80 bands slung over his shoulder.

His next stop was the post office, and then he was hitting I-95.

***

One Week Later

"Shit, girl, where the fuck you learn to suck a dick like that? You suck a dick like you crazy." Rico placed a hand on the back of Ski's head.

She intensely made eye contact with Rico with a mouth full of dick. Rico's manhood was buried deep, coated with Ski's saliva. She slowly worked Rico's manhood to the back of her throat while at the same time humming the hook to Rihanna's song Wild Thoughts that smoothly spilled out of the Benz's speakers.

"Shit!" Rico moaned out, arching his back off the Benz's leather seats.

Ski twirled her head as she sucked hard and strong on Rico's meat.

"Damn, Ski, you gonna make me put this dick in you," Rico mumbled, on his R-Kelly shit as his toes cracked and popped. He was learning firsthand what R-Kelly was feeling by fucking with them young girls. It was something about the young and tender that just made him have to have a piece. Getting some impeccably slow neck from a sweet 16 had Rico worked up.

For the last six months him and Ski had been creeping. He hadn't penetrated her yet, and this fact alone made him feel like he wasn't a creep. He wanted to slide meat into Ski, but he was forcing himself to wait until she was 18.

One night while Tata was out clubbing with her sister and friends, Ski was left at the house. After Rico got out of the shower, he found Ski in his bedroom, lying on his bed with some lace boy shorts with a matching bra on. "What the fuck you doing?" Rico asked, getting angry.

"I can do better than her," Ski said, nodding her head toward the 80-inch Sony TV mounted on the wall.

Rico looked at the TV and seen a beautiful Spanish chick swallowing about a yard of dick. He looked back to Ski in the boy shorts, looking like a young Destiny Moore out the Straight Stunna magazine. Rico's dick rocked up something fierce. He hadn't had an erection like that all year. His dick was fighting to be freed from the towel wrapped around his waist.

Ski hungrily eyed his dick threating to burst through his towel and licked her lips. Rico's eye ran over the curves of her body and went for broke. "Shawty, what can you do with this?" Rico let the towel fall from his body. His dick bounced up and down like a swimming pool diving board.

Ski seductively made her way to the edge of the bed and popped Rico's dick in her mouth like a full-grown woman. She straight-handled her business.

Seven minutes into the best blowjob Rico had in his life, he was on the verge of busting a strong, hard nut. And out of nowhere, Ski stopped, snatching Rico's stick out of her mouth and making the sloppiest slurping sound ever.

Rico froze on his tippy-toes, breathing hard. "What the fuck! Ski, don't stop," Rico begged.

"Uh-huh. Pay me!" Ski protested with her hand out. Rico's dick dangled in front of Ski's pretty face, but she didn't budge.

It was clear to Rico he had been played and had turned a trick in his own house, but the head was too good to just walk away without busting a nut in Ski's mouth. Rico ran over to the dresser, grabbed a stack of bills, and eagerly placed a hundred dollar bill in her hand.

Ski looked at Rico like he shitted on her. "Four more!" Ski demanded, kissing the head of Rico's dick.

Rico was hesitant, but Ski's soft lips encouraged him. He didn't second-guess his actions paying Ski once she put the tip of him in her mouth. Them hundreds rolled outta his hand like dice.

Ski worked her magic, and in two minutes flat Rico exploded in her mouth. Ski came up off Rico's dick and jacked the rest of Rico's seed onto her perky breasts.

Every week from that day on, Rico and Ski had a pay-to-play relationship, which lead them to being in Rico's Benz now.

Rico pumped his hips into Ski's face as thick, white semen shot into her mouth. Ski kept sucking and jacking him until she thought he was empty. Ski came up for air and swallowed hard, sticking her tongue out to show Rico she was a big girl and swallowed.

"Ski, you are a mess," Rico said, chuckling as he put his member back in his Polo jeans.

Ski fixed her hair in the mirror.

"Nah, nigga, I'm not a mess. I'm a fucking beast. Now, let a bitch get hers so I can get up with my nigga," Ski stated in a playful manner, but was dead-ass serious.

Rico couldn't do nothing but shake his head and dig in his pocket. He broke Ski off a couple of bills.

"Thank you, *papi*!" Ski tucked the money in her black Fendi purse.

Rico pulled off the side street and bent a few corners. "The next time we meet up, I think I'm going to beat them guts out. I'm not sure if a nigga can wait until you are 18."

"Shit, *papi*, that's on you. You coulda been gettin' this

pussy, but you trying to be on some modest shit. You need to get this pussy while it's smoking hot," Ski said sexually.

"I know, but I just wanted it to be on my time."

"I hear ya, *papi*," Ski retorted, "but anytime is the right time for me because time is money, and I always got time to make that money. So, here's a little something to motivate you to get with me real soon." Ski lifted up in her seat and eased her pink, lace panties over her hips from under the Gucci skirt she was rockin'.

Rico began to breathe hard. Ski took the panties off and dropped them in Rico's lap. Rico licked his lips as he became bricked in his jeans.

"There go my man, right there, Rico," Ski said, pointing to the white Lexus with the black rims that was sitting on the corner.

Rico pulled up next to the Lexus, and Ski jumped out without giving Rico a goodbye. She ran and jumped in the passenger side of the Lex and tongued her man down. Rico watched in dismay. He wondered if her man tasted his nut on Ski's tongue or smelled him on her breath.

Diego rolled down the Lexus' window. "What it do, Rico?" Diego greeted.

"Ain't too much shaking, slim. Just coolin'. I see you sitting pretty," Rico stated, nodding to the cocaine-white Lexus he was driving.

"What can a nigga say? I'm eating right now, and I got the baddest bitch in the city," Diego boasted.

"I hear ya, slim, and you ain't lyin' about having the baddest chick in the city," Rico retorted, thinking about how he just nutted in Ski's mouth a few blocks away while his lame ass waited on her. "But look, I got some shit to handle, so I'm out."

"A'ight, be easy, slim. And thanks for giving my girl a ride."

"Bye, Uncle Rico! And make sure you got my new number logged in your phone," Ski yelled as Rico pulled off, shaking his head.

Rico picked the pink panties off his lap and smelled the damp crotch of them. Ski's natural scent was intoxicating. He inhaled deeply. "Damn, I got to fuck this little bitch ASAP!" Rico stated to himself as he pushed the panties into his back pocket.

He wondered if Ski got her whorish ways from her mother. They often said the apple don't fall far from the tree.

Rico shook his head at the thought and turned his music up.

Chapter 16

"So, where we going, Diego?" Ski asked, applying some peach-flavored lip-gloss to her lips.

Diego looked over at his eye candy and smiled. He couldn't get over how beautiful she was, and being two years older than her didn't even play a factor in his mind. Her maturity and femininity is what attracted Diego to the young beauty so much. When it came to Ski, it was like a moth drawn to flames. He was dangerously in love with Ski.

"I got to go holla at my Unc about a few things."

"So, I'm finally going to meet D.C.'s infamous Cain, huh?"

"Yup, and while you are there, you need to be on your best behavior."

"Aren't I always?" Ski said playfully.

"Yeah, but sometimes your free spirit qualities can be a bit much."

"Whatever, you just don't know how to have fun. Name one time my free spirit-ness was too much?"

Diego looked at Ski like she was crazy. "I can name one. The time you convinced me to fuck you in your Aunt Tata's bed and she caught us and beat our asses like we was her fucking kids and pointed a gun in my face. I still haven't gotten over that, and the only reason I didn't fuck her ass up is because she is your aunt and I don't hit women."

Ski could hear the anger in her man's voice. "Aw, baby, I'm sorry about that," Ski said, leaning over and placing her lip-gloss on his cheek. "If it make you feel better, we can fuck in your uncle's bed," Ski stated, laughing.

"Yeah, get us both bodied in that bitch," Diego stated seriously. "But after I see my uncle, we going to hit Moe's Crab House. I got a taste for some seafood."

"That's cool, baby. I got all the seafood you can eat right

here, *papi*." Ski lifted her dress up, exposing her neatly-trimmed pussy and playfully batted her naturally-long eyelashes.

Diego bit down on his lip, something he often did when Ski was in her flirtatious state and did something to arouse him. "Damn, bae. If seeing my uncle wasn't a high priority, I would pull the Lex over and straight flex in that pussy," Diego said wiping the excess wetness from his mouth.

"I understand that, Diego, but promise me later you gonna handle this for me," Ski stated, throwing her leg on the dashboard and pulling the lips back on her pussy, brandishing the pinkness of her clit.

"I got you, bae. Don't even trip. I'm going to handle that shit for you real good."

Ski was satisfied with Diego's response. She smiled to herself, pulling her dress down, and found the Cardi B song *Be Careful* on her iPod. She turned the volume up to her liking, got comfortable in the Lexus, and sang along with Cardi B

***

Rico pulled up in the Silver Springs Complex where his soon-to-be baby mom lived. He's been thinking about her a lot lately, especially since the killing of the federal agent. He was wondering what type of father he really could be if he got tapped off in the streets, or even worse, faced a life of incarceration. The thought sent chills through his body. He had to make things right with his future child's mother and tell her about his first babymom, CeCe, and their daughter, Nikki.

Rico shook his head in aggravation at how fucked up his life had become. He still had to deal with the fact he hadn't told Tata about none of his baby mothers.

Rico let out a deep sigh. He moved the fo'-fifth with its red diamond-encrusted handle from under the driver's seat and placed it on his hip. Walking inside the apartment, he was greeted by his swollen-bellied beauty. The white boy shorts she wore were being eaten up by her big pussy lips that threatened to rip through the fabric. Her round melons looked plump and ripe. Her pregnancy was treating her well. It even gave her semi-flat ass a makeover.

"*Hola, papi.* I seen when you pull up, so I thought I'd meet my *papi chulo* at the door like he likes me, half naked and ready to be fucked."

"*Hola, mami.* I love how you be so keen to please me."

"That's my job, to please and honor you. That's what a real woman does. We are getting ready to bring a life into this world together. It's a must we build a solidified bond. That's why it's essential you leave my sister, Tata."

"I know, *mami.* I'm working on that as we speak," Rico confessed.

Tina walked over to Rico, undid his belt buckle, and let his jeans fall to his ankles. She pushed his boxers behind them and fell to her knees. *Damn, the daughter just ate the dick up not even 15 minutes ago, and now the mama getting ready to bless me with some head,* Rico thought to himself and smiled.

Tina got on eye-level with Rico's limp dick. "When you going to leave that bitch?" Tina asked, grabbing ahold of Rico's manhood and slightly starting to stroke him.

"That's in play, *mami,* I promise you."

"What the fuck, nigga!" Tina yelled when she went to jack Rico and a glob of nut oozed out of his dick. Rico looked down and seen the snot-looking substance dripping out of the head of him. "I know you didn't just fuck a bitch and roll up in here with a dirty-ass dick, Rico!" Tina jumped to her feet.

"Come on, *mami,* that ain't nothing but a little pre-cum. You tripping," Rico said, trying to play it off and pull his pants back up.

"Muthafucka, I know pre-cum when I see it, and muthafucka that shit there got babies floating around in it."

"Tina, you on some bullshit! The pregnancy got you tripping hard. I'm going to bounce and holla at you later." Rico turned around to walk out the door.

"What the fuck is this?" Tina asked, snatching a piece of fabric out of his back pocket. She held up a pink pair of panties. Her heart seemed to stop working for about 10 seconds. Her chest squeezed tight like a vice.

Rico stood there with a dumbfounded look on his face, watching the panties dangle between Tina's thumb and index finger. "Fuck!" Rico mumbled.

Tina sprang at Rico like Bengal tiger, nails first. Her nails sunk into his facial skin.

"Argh!" Rico cried out, backhanding Tina to the floor.

Slap!

Tina bounced back up like a human ball. Rico could feel the stinging sensation from the scratches Tina left on his face.

Tina took flight to the bedroom, shouting something in her native tongue that he couldn't understand. Rico went after her, but by the time he made it to the bedroom door, Tina was coming out swinging a metal bat, missing Rico's head by an inch and knocking a chunk of wood out of the doorframe. "Bitch! I'ma kill that ass!" Tina yelled, swinging the bat again, hitting Rico in the shoulder.

Whack! The bat sounded off when making contact with Rico's shoulder. Rico let out a whimpering sound like a dog.

Tina knew she'd hurt him. "You gonna bring your ass!" Tina swung the bat again, missing Rico as he ran out the door. Tina's pregnant ass ran right behind him.

"Hold up, Tina. Let me explain," Rico tried to reason with Tina, but all she saw was red.

Tina chased behind Rico with the bat over her head hoping

she'd get close enough to bust his shit to the white meat. She would be damned if she let him get away with hitting her.

Rico couldn't get in his car without Tina hitting him with the bat, so he ran around his car to get away from her and the wrath of the bat. Tina struggled to catch Rico. The concrete tore into the bottoms of her bare feet, slowing her down.

"Tina, chill the fuck out! You out here making a fucking scene, out here half-ass naked. Look, Tina, everyone is looking at you," Rico pleaded.

Tina's ears were deaf to Rico's reasoning. She knew she couldn't catch him to put a hurting on him, so she destroyed what was dear to him. She drew the bat back and brought it down on the windshield, shattering it. *Bash*! The windshield sounded off. She brought the bat back again and put her weight into it this time. When the bat found home on the windshield, it knocked a hole in it. *Bash*!

Rico was shocked. He wanted to pull the fo'-fifth, but there was too many people outside watching the commotion. Tina went H.A.M. and started beating on the 600 Benz like it was a hooptie. She knocked paint from the car and put volleyball-sized dents in it. Every time she would swing the bat and make contact with the car, Tina's ass cheeks and titties would bounce and jiggle. And with every motion of her goods, the young hustlaz in the complex would cheer her on. And the more damage she caused, the jealous-ass bitches in her complex wanted to beat her ass for wildin'-out on a fine-ass nigga like Rico. But every dope boy who truly knew the value of the 600 cringed with every contact the bat made with the luxury automobile.

Rico finally made it to the driver's side of the car and jumped behind the wheel, locking the door. "Bitch! This shit ain't over, Tina," Rico yelled.

Tina came up on the driver's side, looking like a mad

woman. She swung the bat, shattering the driver's side window. Tiny pieces of broken glass embedded themselves into Rico's face, giving him a face full of tiny cuts to go along with the scratches he already wore.

"Bitch!" Rico said, turning the key in the ignition and snatching the car in reverse. Rico wanted to jump out and murder Tina's ass, but he didn't want to hurt his seed that was growing inside her. So he murdered her with his words. "Fuck you, bitch. That's why Ski's dick sucking skills is better than yours, and Tata's pussy is a hundred times better than your trash-ass pussy."

A different type of anger jumped into Tina. She charged the car. Rico seen her coming and floored the 600. Tina gave chase, but there was no way she was going to catch Rico on foot. In her last attempt to bring Rico some harm, she threw the bat with all her might, trying to hit Rico's car one last time, but she missed by a foot.

Tina fell to her knees, breaking down crying.

Chapter 17

Cain ran a hand over the short hairs sprouting out of the side of his face. He knew he needed a shave, but with Rocco being dead and not knowing who his killer was, he could not allow himself any small pleasures, such as a haircut or shave. It'd been over a month, and not a word had been uttered as to who killed Rocco. Cain even dropped $400,000 as a reward for whoever could lead him to the perpetrators behind his cousin's mysterious murder. Still, no result came out of the reward.

Cain opened his desk drawer and removed a Backwood as big as a Bob Marley spliff. He made sure the cherry on the Backwood was burning evenly before he removed a folded sheet of paper from his desk drawer. Cain took a pull off the Backwood as he locked his brandy-colored eyes on the image on the paper. Cain let out a deep breath along with the smoke he held captured in his lungs. He would give anything to find out who the person in the picture was.

"What's good, Unc?" Diego said, walking into his uncle's office and breaking his trance.

"Problems, and not enough solutions to fix all of them," Cain replied, resting the paper he held in his hand on the desk and taking another toke from the Backwood. Cain stood up and hugged his nephew around the shoulders while keeping his eyes locked on the Latin-looking chick standing in the doorway. She wore a dress that was so short if it raised up just two inches, he would see her love box. What was crazy was the new guest held a look in her eyes like she was familiar with Cain or something.

"And who is the lady?" Cain asked, releasing Diego from their embrace.

"Oh, that's my love, right there, Unc. That's Ski. Her aunt lives down the street from my moms. Ski, this is my unc Cain."

"Hi!" Ski said, batting her long eyelashes.

Cain didn't speak a word. He just nodded his head at Ski, then hit a button on the remote that sat on his desk. "Nephew, I'm going to have your friend wait in the theater while we talk, if that's okay with you."

"That's cool, Unc," Diego said.

On cue, the maid appeared at the door. "Yes, Mr. Cain?"

"Yeah, Hanna. Please escort Ski to the theater and accommodate her with whatever request she makes." He turned to Ski. "I promise I won't keep him long," said Cain, addressing Ski directly for the first time.

Ski walked over and gave Diego a peck on the cheek, then followed the maid out the door. The way Ski's butt jiggled, Cain could tell she didn't have a stitch of drawers on.

Once Diego's company was gone, Cain got serious. "Don't ever in your fucking life bring a bitch to my house unannounced. That shit is pure reckless. Have you forgot that's how Rocco got his shit knocked loose, by bringing a random bitch somewhere she didn't need to be?" Cain stated, looking in Diego's eyes to see if he understood the severity of the mistake he just made.

"Damn, my bad, Unc. I wasn't thinking along those lines. But she's nothing but 16. And she's not even in the streets."

"I don't give a fuck if she is 16 or 26. Trust no bitch. You never know who the fuck that girl knows. This is a small fucking world, and you never know who could be a savage or rubbing elbows with them." Cain was trying to lace his nephew with some game. "And plus, that girl is too young for you. Her ass can bring a lot of trouble on you if the wrong people find out you fucking a minor. What, you on your R-Kelly shit?" Cain questioned.

"Naw, Unc, it's not like that. I understand where you are coming from, and I will take her home soon as we get done here." Diego twisted his fingers together nervously at the intense stare his uncle was giving him.

Cain shook his head, but moved forward with their meeting. He sat back in his Italian leather chair and got comfortable. "I'm assigning you a new work detail." Cain paused to hit the Backwood.

"Okay, that's what I'm talking about!" Diego stated excitedly, rubbing his hands together like they were cold and he was trying to warm them up.

"You going to be groomed under Fate for my top lieutenant spot. Fate is going to be filling Rocco's position as second in command in this business." Diego's expression changed, and Cain picked up on it. "What, you got a problem with that?" Cain questioned Diego.

Diego knew if he didn't express his concerns to his uncle Cain, his uncle would always see him as a do-boy, a common foot soldier. "Unc, I do have a problem with them changes. I mean you no disrespect, but I was hoping I could fulfill Rocco's position. I been putting in work for a minute now. I think it's time for me to really earn my keep and make some real paper." Diego stated, making eye contact with Cain so he could see the seriousness in his eyes.

Cain seen hunger in his nephew's eyes. The hunger pouring out of Diego's eyes was the look of someone who had the overwhelming desire to be a boss. But Cain wasn't doubting Diego could hold Rocco's position. He just thought Diego still had a lot to learn about being a leader.

Cain let out a sigh. "Nephew, I hear where you coming from, and I can see that glare in your eye." Cain hit the Backwood again. "But I can't go on what I see in your eyes to be a boss. It has to be in your heart and in your actions to be a boss. You have to have the ability to feed the people that follow you. To fill Rocco's shoes, you don't just have to be a savage. You have to be a calculated savage."

"And I'm all of that, Unc. Just give me a chance," Diego said, cutting Cain off. "I could run the south side of this city with an iron fist," Diego said with conviction, sitting on the edge of his chair.

Cain looked down at the paper on his desk, and just then a quick idea formulated in the corner of his mind. He pushed the paper toward Diego. "I'm going to make a deal with you, nephew. What you see right there is the tattoo of the bitch who killed Rocco, and if you could locate this bitch, then I will let you take over Rocco's position."

Cain knew Diego would never locate the person in the photo. Cain had every goon and killa in the city trying to secure the large reward money he placed out for the identity of the person in the picture. If Cain's people had come up with nothing, then he knew Diego didn't have a chance of locating the mystery women in the picture.

Diego saw shit for what it was worth. He could see his uncle was trying to set him up for failure. There was no way Diego was going to able to find this woman just based on a tattoo. He saw his uncle was playing him, but he refused to let his uncle see him hurt. "Aye, Unc. I see you think I'm not capable of holding Rocco's spot down. But all I'm asking is for a chance to prove myself."

"And I'm giving you a chance by giving you the task of finding Rocco's killer," Cain said, putting the Backwood out.

The two men locked eyes.

Diego was mad, but he kept his cool. "A'ight, Unc. I'm on it. No problem," Diego said, getting up, scooping up the paper Cain had on his desk, and going to go find Ski.

***

Damn, Tina tried to knock off my shoulder, Rico thought to himself as he massaged the muscle in his shoulder. He laid his Caesar cut on the Uber headrest. He closed his eyes and thought about how Tina straight nutted-up on him about some damn panties. Rico let out a sigh. He needed a blunt and a hot shower to get the stiffness out of his shoulder.

He took his Benz to Big Boyz Toys out in Oxon Hill, Maryland. This was a shop for the top-of-the-line luxury cars. Seeing the true damage Tina did to his car made him want to murder something. Rico knew without a shadow of doubt if he had taken the car home and Tata had seen it, he would have had to kill Tata's ass because she wouldn't let it go until he answered all of her 21 questions. And she would have been screaming that he'd been out there fucking around with another bitch. He refused to have two crazy-ass bitches in his ear.

So he took the car to Big Boyz Toys and caught an Uber home. He was thankful his Uber driver wasn't a talkative one. He enjoyed the sweet melody of Miles Davis that seeped through the car's factory speakers. The jazz was helping calm Rico's nerves.

"We two blocks away from your designation," the Uber driver informed him.

"Cool" Rico replied, still holding his eyes closed.

"What the hell happened here?" the Uber driver spoke out loud.

Rico opened his eyes to see the block where he lived was infested with every type of cop car known to man. His heart kicked hard in his chest like a .44 Mag. in the hand of an inexperienced shooter. Rico could see the SWAT team exiting his house. His mouth became dry. The block was so full of cop cars and F.B.I. agents that the Uber driver couldn't even turn onto his street.

"Keep going!"

Rico's words burst out of him at light speed, scaring the

driver. The Uber driver jumped in her seat and made eye contact with Rico through her rearview mirror. "Sir, I'm only required to take you to your designation."

Rico pulled out his fo'-fifth and placed it to the back of the driver's head. "Bitch, drive the fucking car or this will be your final designation."

Rico pulled out his phone and placed a call.

***

"Can we please have another round?" Tata asked the handsome waiter who kept eye-fucking her. Tonight was girls' night out at Ibiza. It had been a minute since all four women were able to get together due to the paranoia of Rico. Finally Rico let Tata out of his sight, and now they was at club Ibiza on New York Avenue, throwing back a few shots of Peach Ciroc.

They decided to keep it plain. Jeans, button-down designer shirts, and Red Bottoms were the attire for the night.

"Coming right up," the waiter said, sliding his tongue over his bottom lip, trying to get his LL Cool-J on while staring into Tata's eyes.

Tata teased him back and seductively rolled her tongue over her juicy lips, not breaking eye contact with him. The waiter caught a tent in his pants. He eased the notepad he held in front of it, but the women seen it. When he walked away to get their drinks, the women burst out in laughter.

"Oh my God, Tata, you're dead wrong for that," Zoey said, slurping the remainder of her drink through a straw.

"Why you over there playing with that man's emotions? You know damn well you not going to give that nigga some pussy," Jelli chimed in.

"I'm not trying to tease him. I'm just trying to motivate him. If he want a bitch of my character, then he need to come with that bag. I'm not going to lie, though, he is cute as fuck. And it look like he's working with a monster," Tata stated sarcastically, popping her lips.

The women roared in laughter.

"Girl, did you see that fucker's dick print?" Phatmama said, fanning herself and batting her eyes as if she was already head over heels in love with the dick.

"How much you bitches want to bet that nigga coming back and give Tata his number?" Zoey retorted, looking at a dark-skinned dude who walked past their table broadcasting a Colgate smile at her.

"I bet he don't!" Tata said, placing a hundred-dollar bill on the table.

Zoey followed, placing her money on the table.

"We about to find out. Here comes Mr. Lover Boy right now," Phatmama said, smiling at the approaching waiter.

"Here you go, ladies," the waiter said, handing each woman a shot of Peach Ciroc. He did all of this while holding eye contact with Tata and her suckable breasts that were threatening to spill out of her Chanel blouse.

Tata leaned forward and rested her chin on the palm of her hand, looking at the waiter all dreamy-like. It took everything in Jelli not to laugh at Tata's dramatics.

Once again the waiter's flagpole rose, but this time he did nothing to hide his erection. Phatmama got a bad case of the drop-eye. She couldn't keep her eyes off the waiter's dick print

Once Tata broke her dreamy stare and seen his print, she blushed hard. The waiter, being satisfied with Tata getting a peek at what he was slanging, smoothly slid Tata his number and whispered, "Call me." And he walked away.

The ladies once again shared a hearty laugh. "Bitch, I told you he was going to come back with them digits," Zoey said, grabbing the money off the table.

"Okay, what can I say? You know a thirsty nigga when you see one. Now, let's drink up."

Tata's phone vibrated on the table before she could down her drink. She seen it was Rico, and she rolled her eyes and sent him to voicemail. She downed her drink and chased it with a glass of Ace of Spades. Her phone vibrated again. It was Rico calling again. Everything in her told her not to answer the phone, but she went against her instincts. "Hello?"

"Tata, I need you, *mami*," Rico said in a panicked state.

Tata could hear the nervousness in his voice. Her mouth fell open after Rico dropped the unthinkable on her.

"I'll be there in an hour," Tata said into the phone. Her clique could tell something was seriously wrong by the expression Tata wore on her face.

"What's good, *mami*?" Phatmama questioned.

"Shit went down. The feds raided our house."

"What the fuck?" Jelli yelled out, going into a panic and jumping up from her chair. Tata had to yank her by the arm to reseat her.

Zoey placed her face in the palms of her hands and let out a sigh.

"Listen up. This is where shit gets real. Phatmama, you got them burner phones?" Tata asked.

"Yeah, I got some in my truck."

"Alright, here's the game plan," Tata said, getting up and leading the girls outside so they could talk in private.

An hour later, Tata called Rico on the burner phone. "Hello?" Rico's voice came through the phone.

"It's me, *papi*. What room you in? I'm outside," Tata replied.

"Why you calling me from this number?" Rico questioned suspiciously.

"I dropped my phone and cracked the screen, so I had to use one of the burner phones Phatmama gave me."

Rico hesitated. "I'm in room 104," Rico stated and hung up.

The Budget Inn was one of them motels where a person could see the room doors from the parking lot. Tata could see the curtains of 104 slightly move. She knew Rico was watching her. She'd been sitting in the parking lot, watching and taking in the surroundings, making sure shit was safe. Nothing seemed to be out of the ordinary. The motel was located on New York Avenue, a ten-minute drive from club Ibiza where Tata and her clique were having drinks. Tata wanted Rico to think she was an hour away.

Tata and Zoey exited Zoey's truck and found their way to 104. They didn't have to knock. Rico was waiting on them.

Rico had the room dark. Nothing was on but the small TV on the brown wooden dresser. The TV was on the news. Fox 5 was broadcasting anything and everything about the McCormick & Smith jewelry heist, the murder of the off-duty F.B.I. agent, and the raid of Rico Johnson's house. They flashed a picture of him on the screen.

Rico's clothes were in disarray, and the stress lines attacked his forehead like stretch marks attack a fat girl's stomach. The room air was stale and stuffy from lack of ventilation and cigarette smoke.

"Rico, what the fuck is going on?" Tata asked Rico as she hugged him.

Rico looked toward Zoey as if he didn't want to talk in front of her, and Tata caught on. "She in it with us, so you can speak in front of her."

He didn't really want to, but Rico started talking. "I came up to the house, and when I got there, police was everywhere, I mean, SWAT and the feds was there. Shit, the whole fucking task force was there." Rico started pacing the floor. "I don't know how they got onto me about the heist and the murder of the agent, but shit is fucked up. We got to get ghost, Tata."

"Ok, *papi*. What's your thoughts?"

"I think maybe Tone or Diesel put them folks on me. I been blowing Diesel's phone up all night, and he ain't answer yet. But I'm really thinking it was Tone. He was bitter about how shit went down with us," Rico stated, stopping in the middle of the room to light another Newport.

Zoey heard this and shook her head in disappointment. All this shit could have been avoided if Rico would have given Tone a few bands so he could lay low after the fed shooting.

"It could have been any of them, but right now we need to put some distance in between us and them feds so we can gather our thoughts and see what our next move going to be," Tata retorted, pulling an ounce of loud out of her pocket and tossing it to Rico with a pack of Backwoods. She was careful not to touch anything in the room.

"This what I need you to do, Tata. I need you to go to this address and empty out the safe and grab the jewelry from the McCormick & Smith heist. Then I want you to go take the jewels and meet Rau'f and trade them for cash. I already touched bases with Rau'f. He is going to meet you once you grab the goods and give me a call," Rico said, texting Tata's burner phone with all the info she needed. "You should be back here in no less than two hours, tops. Don't make no pit stops. Get the money at the apartment first, and then go meet Rau'f. After that, get the fuck back here so we can get the fuck out of here," Rico said, putting his phone in his back pocket.

"Okay, *papi*, me and Zoey is on it. What about Phatmama and Jelli?" Tata asked, kissing Rico on the lips and walking to the door.

"Don't tell them bitches shit. We gonna reach out to them once we get to where we going," Rico replied, not making eye contact with Tata.

Tata could tell Rico was lying. He had no plans to inform Jelli and Phatmama of the current situation or even have them meet up with them later on down the line.

"Okay, *papi*. We out. See you in a few," Tata said, leaving out the door with Zoey behind her.

She loved when a plan came together.

Jibril Williams

Chapter 18

"Can you please at least tell me what's bothering you?" Ski asked with an attitude. Ever since Diego met with his uncle, he'd been mean and distant. Whatever Cain met with him about, it must have been bad.

"Ain't nothing wrong, Ski. I just got a lot of shit on my mind. I just need some time to think things through."

"Well, at least could you take me to Moe's Crab House like you told me we was going to after we left your uncle's house?" Ski rolling her beautiful eyes at Diego.

Diego reached into his pocket, pulled a few bills off his bankroll, and handed them to Ski. "Order some takeout."

Ski snatched the money from Diego, trying to get a reaction out of him, but it failed.

Diego knew he was wrong for acting the way he was toward Ski, but his Uncle had him deep in his mind. Never in a million years he would've thought Cain would send him on a dummy mission because he felt he couldn't handle a certain task. Diego was really feeling like Cain was testing his gangsta. To make matters worse, he felt like Cain was choosing Fate over him. All these years Cain preached family over everything, so for him to choose Fate to fulfill Rocco's position over him was a slap in the face to Diego. It made Cain look like a hypocrite in his eyes.

Diego pulled his Lexus up in front of Ski's mother's apartment complex. "I'm going to holla at you later, bae," Diego said, leaning over and kissing Ski on the cheek.

Ski opened the car door, but stopped midway. She grabbed Diego's hand. "Diego, whatever you going through, just know I'm with you through it all. I'm your ride-or-die. Please don't shut me out," Ski said sincerely.

Diego nodded his head up and down in respect to Ski's statement. To be honest, her words touched him in a special kinda way.

Ski got out of the car and made her way inside her mother's two-bedroom apartment that they shared together. Ski found her mother sitting on the couch, staring into space with tears coming down her cheeks. "*Hola*, Mama. Are you alright?" Ski asked, going to her mother's side and putting an arm around her.

She knew her mom was having a hard time having a baby 16 years after her first child, and to make the situation even worse, Tina's current baby daddy was a deadbeat because he hadn't even shown his face around the apartment. Well, that was Ski's perception, anyway.

"I'm ok, Ski. I will be alright," Tina replied, drying tears with the back of her hands. Tina badly wanted to ask her daughter about fucking with Rico, but she couldn't bring herself to do it because she would expose the fact her and Rico was fucking around behind Tata's back. *Your daughter suck dick better than you!* Those words kept echoing in Tina's head. She didn't know why those words bothered her so much. All she knew was Rico said them with so much malice in them.

"Is there anything I could do, Mama?" Ski asked, rubbing her mother's hand, trying to comfort her.

"No, Ski. I'm fine."

"Well, let me order us some dinner. Does steak and baked potatoes sound good?"

"That would be fine." Tina wiped snot from her running nose.

Ski kissed her mother on the cheek and got up to call in their order. "Ma, why you got my panties in the middle of the floor?" Ski said, picking up the pink panties that rested by the front door.

Tina had never in her life been hit by a truck, but once Ski acknowledge the panties as her very own, it felt like she'd been hit by an 18-wheeler. She began to feel hot and dizzy. Her breathing became troubled. She closed her eyes and fought to compose herself.

"It musta fell out the dirty clothes bag when I went to do laundry earlier," Tina said with tears leaking from her eyes.

***

Zoey pulled up to the Lexus dealership in Silver Spring, Maryland. This was one of Rau'f's legit business establishments. Tata checked her Glock and slipped it on her hip. She checked her surroundings. Shit looked kosher.

"Listen, Zoey. When we go in here, let me do all the talking. You just be on point. We can't trust no one at this point."

Zoey nodded her head in agreement as she checked her clip on her own Glock that held 30 rounds. Tata and Zoey made their way inside the dealership. There weren't many people inside. It was getting late, and the sun had already gone down.

They were met by Rau'f's bodyguard, Fidel. "Here to see Rau'f?" the slim-built, sinewy-looking guy asked. Tata nodded her head up and down. "Follow me, miss," Fidel said, leading the way to a side room. Zoey tensed up upon seeing another man standing in the room holding an Uzi. "I'm sorry, but we have to search you and take your weapons, if you have any," Fidel said, stepping forward.

"Fuck nawl, we ain't giving up our weapons," Tata protested.

"Then you don't get to see Rau'f," Fidel said firmly.

Tata was uncomfortable with disarming herself in this type of setting. She had to make a choice fast. She leaned over and whispered in Zoey ear. "If I'm not out with the money or jewels in 15 minutes, come in this bitch blazing," Tata ordered, handing Zoey her Glock.

Zoey hesitated, but she respected the first part of the oath. "When one leads, the others follow." Plus, Zoey loved to get it poppin'. She placed Tata's gun in the small of her back. "Fifteen minutes, *mami*, and I'm coming in for you," Zoey stated seriously while looking dead at Fidel, who stood there unfazed.

Zoey dropped the black bag from her shoulders and handed it to Tata, then stepped back through the door she came from and found herself back on the Lexus showroom floor.

Tata handed over her phone. Fidel handed the phone over to the gunman holding the Uzi, who powered the phone off and placed it in his pocket.

Fidel quickly went through the bag and gave it back to Tata. He pat-searched Tata and led her through another door where Rau'f was waiting on her and watching everything that transpired on a monitor.

"*Salaam*," *peace*, he greeted. "Tata, what a pleasure to see you again," Rau'f said, standing up and kissing here soft chocolate hand.

"Hey, Rau'f. Glad to see you, too, but not under these circumstances."

"I'm well aware of the current situation." Rau'f said, stroking his beard.

Rau'f was Moroccan and made millions on the black market selling and buying diamonds and white gold. Many thought Rau'f was just a successful businessman due to him having several businesses throughout D.C., Maryland, and Virginia. Rico thought it was the diamonds that motivated Rau'f, but he was far from being right. It was the white gold that was worth a fortune in Morocco. What Rico didn't know was Rau'f owned an import and export business that smuggled high-quality drugs into the country and shipped millions of United States currency out of the country.

Rau'f was the plan type. Nothing about him was flashy except the white gold Yacht Master diamond Rolex he sported. His attire was reminiscent of someone who was out to play golf. His khaki pants and button-down Polo shirt gave Rau'f the look of a man who was enjoying a vacation, but his walnut-colored eyes had a wariness to them, telling a story that he had seen more evil shit than any street nigga had ever seen. The 357 Rhino he kept tucked on his waistline was a confession to that.

Even though Rau'f was in his mid-50s and wore 157 pounds, he was light on his feet and quick to judge. His skin was cocoa-brown, and he hid his Moroccan accent well. Most people would think he was born in the United States.

"I know you are pressed for time, so let me see what you've got," Rau'f stated, laying a black velvet cloth on top of the glass desk.

Tata began emptying out the book bag. Rau'f sat back with a poker face, but inside he was smiling hard as Tata placed Rolex watch after Rolex watch on the velvet cloth. He knew he was going to see some good money back home for the five white gold Presidential Rolexes alone.

When Tata finished placing the merchandise on the table, it was five Presidential Rolexes, four Yacht Masters, six Oyster Perpetual Air Kings, two Celines, three Daytonas with white and blue diamond bezels, and nine Cartier Pashas with emerald dials. Rau'f wasn't even paying too much attention to the miscellaneous ankle and tennis bracelets. He was focused on the watches. They were big sellers in Morocco.

Rau'f picked a few pieces up and examined them. He reached for the phone that rested at the corner of the glass desk. He pushed a button and spoke into the phone. "365," was all Rau'f said into the phone before he hung up.

"The money will be here shortly," Rau'f said, adjusting the Rhino on his hip and removing a Cuban cigar from the drawer of the glass desk. He quickly clipped the ends of the cigar and blazed it. He took a few puffs to get the highly-loved cigar burning evenly.

Tata took in the room for the first time. Even though there wasn't much in the room, for some reason it felt like money. The glass desk looked to be worth thousands. Tata had never seen a desk strictly made of glass. The glass seemed to be high quality. Three Dell computers rested on the desktop, and two matching leather chairs sat in front of Rau'f's desk. The chairs were of expensive leather, the kind that could only be found by hand-picking the material in Italy.

"The circumstances of the situation are a grave matter," Rau'f said, breaking the silence.

"It is, and we appreciate you meeting with us on short notice." Tata spoke and showing her gratitude.

Rau'f let a cloud of smoke out of his mouth. The cigar smoke quickly filled the room. "I wasn't too keen on meeting up with Rico after he broke the situation down to me, but once he told me he was sending you, I couldn't deny seeing a goddess in the flesh. It's not every day you get to see one."

Tata blushed. "I bet you tell all the women that same line," she said, shifting her weight from her right leg to the left.

"Is there a chance you could accompany me to dinner?" Rau'f asked, ignoring Tata's comment.

"Listen, Rau'f. I'm about business. I'm not about opening my legs for a few dollars. I got some merchandise I need to get off. Are you willing to do business with me?" Tata said, putting it all out there that she wasn't his average bitch. She was a boss in her own right.

Rau'f burst out laughing, making Tata feel a certain way. "I can't fucking believe it. Rico told me you pulled off that black diamond heist, but I didn't believe him. But I do now, since you are in my face talking about having some merchandise you want to get rid of."

"Don't fucking sleep on me and my girls," Tata said, checking her Cartier. She was cutting it close with the 15 minutes she gave Zoey.

A knock came at the door, and Fidel walked in, placed a Gucci travel bag on the desk, and walked out. Tata opened the bag and bundles of money wrapped with red rubber bands looked back at her. She closed the bag and started walking to the door.

"I'm interested in seeing the merchandise you have," Rau'f said, watching Tata's backside as he blew Os in the air.

"We can link up. I already got your number."

"But you never answered my question. Will you accompany me to dinner?"

"I'm sorry, Rau'f. I don't mix business with pleasure. But I will be in touch, though," Tata said, exiting the room and finding herself face-to-face with the Uzi-clutching gunman who led her to the door that exited out onto the showroom floor.

When she found Zoey and Fidel, he handed her back her phone. Tata didn't extend her goodbyes to Fidel. She exited the Lexus dealership with Zoey following close behind. Tata's mind was on their next mission.

Chapter 19

Tata fished the burner phone out of her pocket while Zoey maneuvered through traffic as if they were on a casual drive through the city. The large sum of money they had emptied out of Rico's safe and the money they got from Rau'f rested on the back seat.

The phone rang twice before a voice came through the other end of the phone. "Hello."

"Diesel, this Tata. Have you heard?"

"This shit is all over the fucking news. They talking about Rico wanted for killing the agent in connection with the jewelry store heist," Diesel stated in a panicked tone.

"I saw the same shit. Have you heard from Rico?" Tata asked, but already knew her answer.

"This nigga been blowing my phone up non-stop, but I'm not answering at this moment. I need to put some distance between me and him."

Just like a scared-ass nigga, Tata thought. *When a little heat come down on their partner, the first thing a nigga do is abandon ship.* "I understand, Diesel."

"We need to link up, Tata."

"I know we do, bae, but I'm handling some shit right now. I'm assuming the feds didn't show up at your doorstep?"

"It's been quiet on this end."

"So, it's safe to say you might not be on their radar," Tata asked, adjusting the Glock that lay between her legs.

"Yeah, you got a point, but I'm not taking no chances. I'm wondering how they got onto Rico?" Diesel asked.

"Tone's bitch-ass put them peoples on Rico."

Diesel was quiet for a minute. He was thankful he had given Tone that 30 bands so he could get out of town. "I was thinking the same thing," Diesel confirmed.

"Diesel, I'm going to hit you in a few hours. Stay on point. I'm trying to locate Rico. When I talk to him, I will let you know," Tata said.

"Okay, cool. Be careful, and I love you."

"Likewise," Tata said, ending the call.

Tata placed another call. Phatmama picked up on the first ring. "You ready?" Tata said into the phone once Phatmama answered.

"Can't wait. We en route."

That's all that was said before both parties hung up.

Tata and Zoey pulled back into the Budget Inn parking lot. Tata sent Rico a text, informing him they were on their way to the room and to open the door. She could see the curtain move and knew Rico was watching them. Zoey and Tata's eyes scanned the parking lot. A few prostitutes walked tricks to their rooms to make a living on their backs, but other than that, everything was quite.

When Tata and Zoey reached Rico's door, just like last time, they didn't have to knock. He opened the door for them. Once they came into the room, Rico held the door ajar and scanned the parking lot. He held his custom made fo'-fifth in his hand. Feeling comfortable that everything looked kosher, he closed the door.

"Everything went well with Rau'f. He gave me $365,000 for the goods," Tata said, sitting on the edge of the bed.

Zoey dropped the money from Rico's stash and Rau'f on the small, round table that sat in the corner of the room. The TV was on the news. They weren't talking about the whereabouts of Rico, but about a string of killings that had taken place throughout the D.C., Maryland, and Virginia area in the past few months. The victims were known drug dealers. The killer had done some sick, sadistic acts with the victims' private parts.

Rico went over to the bags and examined the money. He

was satisfied with what he saw. He was ready to make his getaway. He dialed Diesel's number, and it went straight to voicemail. He placed his phone in his back pocket.

Rico was moving funny. He hadn't looked at Tata one time since she came back from meeting Rau'f.

With one swift motion, Rico pointed the fo'-fifth at Zoey. "Bitch, lay the fuck on the bed," Rico spoke in a devilish tone.

"Rico, what the fuck you doing, *papi*," Tata questioned in shock, easing her hand toward her Glock.

"I'm sorry, *mami*. You and this bitch gotta go. I gotta get in the wind, and I can't leave no loose ends."

"Come on, *papi*. We not a problem. We family, *papi*. All the shit we done."

"Fuck that. The feds on my ass. I'm—"

The knock at the door caught Rico by surprise just enough for Zoey to catch him with a crisp two-piece that sent him stumbling back against the door as he lost his grip on his gun. Tata upped her Glock with lightning speed and swung the gun sideways. The gun made contact with Rico's jawline.

Crack! A pain shot from Rico's jaw up to his eardrum.

Zoey pulled her own Glock. "Bitch, you was going to kill me," Zoey said, breathing hard, pointing her Glock with fire in her eyes.

The knocks at the door came harder and more rapid. Tata grabbed Rico by his AirMax and pulled him away from the door. Rico lay there, dizzy and with his thoughts discombobulated.

"Get the door, Zoey," Tata ordered. She stood over Rico, pointing her gun at him with two hands.

Zoey scooped Rico's gun up and opened the door just in time to catch Phatmama with her foot midair, getting ready to kick the door in, with Jelli standing behind her with her gun out, ready to let her Glock bark.

"What the fuck?" Phatmama said, rushing into the room. "I heard something bang up against the door. I thought it was going down in this bitch." Phatmama stopped, seeing Rico lying on the floor, clutching his grill.

Jelli came in and Zoey closed and locked the door behind her.

"This nigga was going to kill us," Tata barked.

"Naw, *mami*, I was just fucking wit' y'all," Rico spoke through the pain throbbing in his jaw.

"You lying, bitch-ass nigga. Let's get this party started," Tata informed her girls.

Jelli dropped the duffle bag she had strapped over her shoulders. She reached into the bag and came out with a pair of zip ties. She secured Rico's hands behind his back. Tata removed Rico's AirMaxes and black Billionaire jeans and boxers. Phatmama placed a ball gag in Rico's mouth.

The women worked as a team. Rico tried to resist, but Phatmama slapped him viciously, sending more pain up Rico's jaw. Rico came into compliance and let Phatmama fill his mouth with the ball gag, securing the straps in the back behind his head.

Rico didn't know if his jaw was broken or not, but the pain he felt in his jaw made him lightheaded. Sweat was starting to formulate on his forehead. He was wondering why these bitches had him naked from the waist down. "Hum hum," Rico tried to speak, but the ball gag prevented him from doing so. Still, he tried. "Hum hum!" Nothing was intelligible coming out of his mouth.

"Shh!" Phatmama instructed him.

The four women stood around, watching Rico squirm. They all knew what had to be done. Rico left Tone out to dry, which forced Tone to betray Rico. This, though, wasn't concrete with the women. It could have been Diesel who tipped off the feds.

But one thing was for sure: the women weren't taking no chances. They were cleaning house. Going back to prison wasn't an option.

"Phatmama, grab a pair of grip pliers out of the duffle bag. The kind when you squeeze them around something, they latch onto it." She also removed four steel axes and her trusty blowtorch.

Rico started screaming and going wild. He tried to double-foot kick Phatmama with both ankles that were tied together. The women wrestled his legs down and tied them together at the kneecaps. Rico began to cry hysterically, bubbles of snot forming out of his nose. He looked so weak and fragile. His chest heaved. Fear poured down his face, but the women held no mercy in their eyes. They were all intent on what they had to do.

Each woman grabbed an axe. The light from the TV gleamed off their stainless steel axes, giving their weapons a grim, menacing look that frightened Rico so bad he broke wind, filling the small motel room with a toxic odor.

"What the fuck?" Zoey said, scrunching her face up. Jelli covered her nose.

Phatmama inhaled deeply. "That's pure fear you smelling," Phatmama replied.

Tata didn't say a word at first. She was mentally gearing herself up for what she had to do. Finally, she let out a deep breath. "Rico, how does it feel to be at someone else's mercy?" Tata finally spoke.

Rico tried to reply. "Hum-huh argh." But none of the women wanted to hear what he had to say, so no one made the effort to remove the ball gag from his mouth.

"The first part of the oath. I lead, you follow?" Tata asked. All three women nodded in sync.

Tata drew the axe overhead and brought it down across

Rico's ankle, which was easily severed from the rest of his body.

Rico let out a muffled howl that was unreal. "Grr! Grr!" Blood poured from the bottom of his leg like running water.

Phatmama followed Tata's lead by bringing her axe down above Rico's kneecap, but she wasn't as successful as Tata at severing Rico's limb from his body. The axe was embedded in Rico's femur bone. Blood splashed all over the walls from the gaping gash. The wet, sticky liquid splattered upon Phatmama, soaking her shirt, but she was unfazed. She was used to having blood on her hands. This was right within her element.

"Grr!" Rico hollered. He bit down on the gag ball so hard he broke one of his front teeth. Blood pumped out of his limbs endlessly. His body shook and he passed out. Jelli slung the axe above her head and slammed it down into Rico's thigh. Like Phatmama's, her axe became embedded in Rico's leg.

Rico squirmed like he was summoned from a nightmare. "Grr! Argh!" He quivered and twisted hard in his restraints.

Tata placed one of her Red Bottoms on Rico's neck, holding him still while Jelli worked her axe free from him. The axe released from Rico's leg with a wet, sick, mushy sound. Jelli gave the axe another swing, cutting the thick part of Rico's thigh, finally going through his femur with a loud, snapping sound.

Rico let out a wail the gag couldn't contain. He started to shake profusely and his eyes rolled into the back of his head.

"Naw, nigga, you ain't going to die before I give you mines," Zoey said, bringing her axe down into the center of Rico's chest.

Rico instantly stopped breathing.

The four women took turns chopping Rico's body up into pieces. They only spared his head. The room looked like it was straight out of a horror movie. Blood and bone matter was everywhere. The women's clothes were a mess. Tata and Jelli and Zoey went into the bathroom to clean up as much as they could while Phatmama went to work on what was left of Rico. She grabbed her blowtorch and turned it up high. She put the scorching heat to Rico's dick and nuts, frying it to a fricking seed.

Phatmama started bleaching the room down. Tata, Jelli, and Zoey came out of the bathroom looking a little cleaner and took on the task of bleaching the room down while Phatmama went into the bathroom to clean herself up. The bleach made it hard to breath. They had to cover their noses with shirts to keep from becoming overwhelmed by the fumes from the bleach.

Fifteen minutes later with everything bleached down and axes wiped clean, the four women made their way out of the motel room as if nothing had happened, their Red Bottoms clacking against the parking lot concrete.

Chapter 20

Nine Days Later

Diego must have looked at the photo his Uncle Cain had given him of Rocco's killer a thousand times. The woman who wore the super big and extra dark Gucci shades was hard to identify. Her shades took up most of her face, and with the big hat she wore, it didn't make it any easier to see who she really was.

Diego flipped to the next photo of the killer's tattoo. The she-devil looked wicked, holding the two-large revolver in its hand. The she-devil itself seemed to be smirking at Diego. "Everybody think I'm a fucking joke," said Diego.

Cain had given him a proposition: find this person in the photo to secure his cousin Rocco's spot as second-in-command in Cain's organization, or continue to be a foot soldier. Those really weren't Cain's exact words, but that's how Diego was taking them.

Tap-tap! Ski's manicured nails tapping the window brought Diego out of his daydream. He leaned over and put the photos in his glove compartment, then unlocked the car door and let Ski in. "Hey, bae!" Diego said, greeting the love of his life. "Where your moms? She ain't going?"

"Hey, Diego. She already left. She didn't want to ride with us. She been acting really strange toward me lately, so I just been giving my moms her space. All she been doing is crying for no reason," Ski replied.

"It just may be the pregnancy, Ski."

"Yeah, maybe, but I hope she get it together soon, because she's getting on my fucking nerves, looking at me all fucking crazy and shit. I don't have time for all of that." Ski balled her face up and rolled her eyes.

Diego just chuckled and eased the Lexus out of Ski's

complex's parking lot. "Fire that blunt up in the ashtray," Diego instructed Ski. He turned the volume up on the Bose stereo and the lyrics of Shy Glizzy seeped through his speakers.

Ski lit the blunt and took a few needed pulls of it. She was nervous about going to Rico's funeral. She let the smoke ease out through her nose.

Diego could see his baby was stressed. "You alright over there?"

"Yeah, I'm good," Ski replied, passing him the blunt. "Thanks for going to Rico's funeral with me."

"It's all good. What would I look like, not supporting my bae at her most critical time of need?" Diego stated, switching lanes and hitting the blunt.

They both fell into their own world for a brief moment until Ski broke the silence. "That's crazy how housekeeping at the Budget Inn found Rico's body all chopped up with his head sitting in the middle of the bed," Ski said out of nowhere, shutting her eyes and shaking her head from left to right.

"Whoever did that shit went straight Friday the 13th on Rico's ass."

Ski's eyes popped open, and she looked at Diego like he was crazy.

"I'm sorry, bae. A nigga was a little insensitive with that comment."

"A little isn't the word. Geez, Diego."

"My, bad, Ski," Diego said, checking his mirrors and placing his hand on her thigh. "Do you think Rico killed that Uber driver they found dead in her car behind the Budget Inn?"

"Well, according to the news, the Uber driver was supposed to drive someone to Rico's address, but she never clocked in saying she made it to the designation. So, most likely Rico took an Uber to the house, seen the police, and made the Uber driver take him to the Budget Inn on New York Avenue. But who really knows, though," Ski said, sighing.

Diego pulled up at the funeral home on Good Hope Road. If Ski didn't know any better, she would have thought she was rolling up to a block party. Everyone and their mother came out to send Rico away.

When Ski seen Tata get out of Zoey's truck, her breath got caught in her throat. "Diego, when the funeral is over, I got something I need to tell you about Rico's death."

***

Tata sat on the passenger side of Zoey's QX-6O. She'd been playing the grieving girlfriend since the police informed her Rico's body was found at the motel. Just to play the roll correctly, she made it her business to send Rico out in style. That was the least she could do, since after counting the money from Rico's stash and the money she got from Rau'f, she was sitting on $623,000.

"Let's go," Tata said, throwing her Prada shades on and exiting the truck. Zoey followed suit. Jelli and Phatmama got out of their car that was parked next to Zoey's truck. The four women made their way inside the funeral home.

The place was packed. Everyone wore said faces. Tata and her team made it down to the front of the funeral home where Rico's casket rested. There wasn't nothing to see inside the pearl-white casket due to the dismantling of Rico's body. It was best to have a closed casket. A single picture sat on top of the casket. It was a face shot of Rico baring a million-dollar smile.

Making it to Rico's casket, Tata was thrown off by how her sister Tina was carrying on. She was laying over Rico's casket, bawling her eyes out. "Oh, Rico. I'm sorry, baby," Tina cried.

That statement had Tata looking at her crazy. Tata walked up beside Tina and tried to console her. Tina took one look at

Tata and yanked away from her roughly. Tina looked at Tata with hate in her eyes.

"What the fuck!" Phatmama mumbled under her breath. For a minute she thought Tina was going to swing on Tata.

Tina turned back to Rico's casket, wiping her tears with the heels of her hands, and placed a kiss on the lid of his casket, leaving a deep red lipstick imprint of her lips behind. Tina turned and went to sit in the first pew.

Tata made a mental note to check Tina's ass later. Tata laid a red rose on top of Rico's casket and took a seat next to a grieving Tina. Phatmama, Zoey, and Jelli also sat in the front row. Many came to pay their respects. Rau'f even came through with his bodyguard, Fidel.

Ski came in next with her boyfriend. Ski didn't even make eye contact with Tata or her mother. Tata wondered why both of these bitches was acting stupid.

Diego locked eyes with the big-boned chick who sat next to Ski's aunt Tata. Phatmama thought the stud was admiring her and gave him a look like, *Boy, you are too young. I'll fuck your young ass under the table.*

Ski and Diego took a seat in the second row behind Tata. Ski held Diego's hand for comfort. Diego squeezed Ski's hand hard.

"Ouch, Diego!"

"I'm sorry," Diego said, realizing he was hurting Ski's hand.

"Are you okay?" Ski questioned.

"I just need some air," Diego stated, getting up and walking out as the preacher started to deliver his 'going home' speech for Rico.

Once the preacher began to talk, everything was a blur for Tata. She couldn't remember anything the man said about Rico. The ride to Harmony Cemetery was short, and saying goodbye to Rico and putting him in the ground was even shorter. Once everyone was gone, Tata and her clique remained standing at Rico's grave. All four women hawked spit into Rico's grave, giving him his last due respect.

Zoey's truck and Jelli's car sat waiting by a Red Dodge Charger. Two black GMC trucks pulled up with dark tints. Four goon-looking men got out of the trucks and started walking toward Phatmama.

The women seen them coming. Tata felt something wasn't right. The men didn't look like they were the feds.

Phatmama's hand dropped to the small of her back. One of the approaching men removed a gun from his hip. Phatmama was pulling her Glock at the same time.

Everything went into slow motion as hell erupted in Harmony Cemetery.

Boom! Boom! Boom!

Blocka–blocka–blocka!

Tata's face hit the cemetery dirt.

To Be Continued…
The Heart of a Savage 2
Coming Soon

Submission Guideline

Submit the first three chapters of your completed manuscript to ldpsubmissions@gmail.com, subject line: Your book's title. The manuscript must be in a .doc file and sent as an attachment. Document should be in Times New Roman, double spaced and in size 12 font. Also, provide your synopsis and full contact information. If sending multiple submissions, they must each be in a separate email.

Have a story but no way to send it electronically? You can still submit to LDP/Ca$h Presents. Send in the first three chapters, written or typed, of your completed manuscript to:

LDP: Submissions Dept
Po Box 870494
Mesquite, Tx 75187

DO NOT send original manuscript. Must be a duplicate.

Provide your synopsis and a cover letter containing your full contact information.

Thanks for considering LDP and Ca$h Presents.

The Heart of a Savage

Jibril Williams

A HUSTLER'S DECEIT 3

KILL ZONE **II**

BAE BELONGS TO ME III

SOUL OF A MONSTER II

By **Aryanna**

THE COST OF LOYALTY **III**

By **Kweli**

SHE FELL IN LOVE WITH A REAL ONE **II**

By **Tamara Butler**

RENEGADE BOYS **III**

By **Meesha**

CORRUPTED BY A GANGSTA **IV**

By **Destiny Skai**

A GANGSTER'S SYN II

By **J-Blunt**

KING OF NEW YORK V

RISE TO POWER III

COKE KINGS II

By **T.J. Edwards**

GORILLAZ IN THE BAY III

De'Kari

THE STREETS ARE CALLING II

Duquie Wilson

KINGPIN KILLAZ IV

STREET KINGS 2

PAID IN BLOOD 2

Hood Rich

SINS OF A HUSTLA II

ASAD

TRIGGADALE II

Elijah R. Freeman

MARRIED TO A BOSS III

By Destiny Skai & Chris Green

KINGS OF THE GAME III

Playa Ray

SLAUGHTER GANG II

By Willie Slaughter

THE HEART OF A SAVAGE

By Jibril Williams

<u>**Available Now**</u>

<u>RESTRAINING ORDER **I & II**</u>

By **CA$H & Coffee**

<u>LOVE KNOWS NO BOUNDARIES **I II & III**</u>

By **Coffee**

<u>RAISED AS A GOON I, II, III & IV</u>

<u>BRED BY THE SLUMS I, II, III</u>

<u>BLAST FOR ME I & II</u>

<u>ROTTEN TO THE CORE I III</u>

<u>A BRONX TALE I, II, III</u>

<u>DUFFEL BAG CARTEL I II III</u>

By **Ghost**

<u>LAY IT DOWN **I & II**</u>

Jibril Williams

LAST OF A DYING BREED

BLOOD STAINS OF A SHOTTA I & II

By **Jamaica**

LOYAL TO THE GAME

LOYAL TO THE GAME II

LOYAL TO THE GAME III

LIFE OF SIN I, II

By **TJ & Jelissa**

BLOODY COMMAS I & II

SKI MASK CARTEL I II & III

KING OF NEW YORK I II,III IV

RISE TO POWER I II

COKE KINGS

By **T.J. Edwards**

IF LOVING HIM IS WRONG…I & II

LOVE ME EVEN WHEN IT HURTS I II

By **Jelissa**

WHEN THE STREETS CLAP BACK I & II III

By **Jibril Williams**

A DISTINGUISHED THUG STOLE MY HEART I II & III

LOVE SHOULDN'T HURT I II III IV

RENEGADE BOYS I & II

By **Meesha**

A GANGSTER'S CODE I &, II III

A GANGSTER'S SYN

By **J-Blunt**

PUSH IT TO THE LIMIT

The Heart of a Savage

By **Bre' Hayes**

BLOOD OF A BOSS **I, II, III, IV, V**

By **Askari**

THE STREETS BLEED MURDER **I, II & III**

THE HEART OF A GANGSTA I II& III

By **Jerry Jackson**

CUM FOR ME

CUM FOR ME 2

CUM FOR ME 3

CUM FOR ME 4

An **LDP Erotica Collaboration**

BRIDE OF A HUSTLA **I II & II**

THE FETTI GIRLS **I, II& III**

CORRUPTED BY A GANGSTA I, II & III

By **Destiny Skai**

WHEN A GOOD GIRL GOES BAD

By **Adrienne**

THE COST OF LOYALTY

By Kweli

A GANGSTER'S REVENGE **I II III & IV**

THE BOSS MAN'S DAUGHTERS

THE BOSS MAN'S DAUGHTERS II

THE BOSSMAN'S DAUGHTERS III

THE BOSSMAN'S DAUGHTERS IV

THE BOSS MAN'S DAUGHTERS **V**

A SAVAGE LOVE **I & II**

BAE BELONGS TO ME I II

Jibril Williams

A HUSTLER'S DECEIT I, II, III

WHAT BAD BITCHES DO I, II, III

SOUL OF A MONSTER

By **Aryanna**

A KINGPIN'S AMBITON

A KINGPIN'S AMBITION **II**

I MURDER FOR THE DOUGH

By **Ambitious**

TRUE SAVAGE

TRUE SAVAGE II

TRUE SAVAGE **III**

TRUE SAVAGE **IV**

TRUE SAVAGE **V**

TRUE SAVAGE **VI**

By **Chris Green**

A DOPEBOY'S PRAYER

By **Eddie "Wolf" Lee**

THE KING CARTEL **I, II & III**

By **Frank Gresham**

THESE NIGGAS AIN'T LOYAL **I, II & III**

By **Nikki Tee**

GANGSTA SHYT **I II &III**

By **CATO**

THE ULTIMATE BETRAYAL

By **Phoenix**

BOSS'N UP **I , II & III**

By **Royal Nicole**

I LOVE YOU TO DEATH

By Destiny J

I RIDE FOR MY HITTA

I STILL RIDE FOR MY HITTA

By **Misty Holt**

LOVE & CHASIN' PAPER

By **Qay Crockett**

TO DIE IN VAIN

SINS OF A HUSTLA

By **ASAD**

BROOKLYN HUSTLAZ

By **Boogsy Morina**

BROOKLYN ON LOCK I & II

By **Sonovia**

GANGSTA CITY

By **Teddy Duke**

A DRUG KING AND HIS DIAMOND I & II III

A DOPEMAN'S RICHES

HER MAN, MINE'S TOO I, II

CASH MONEY HO'S

By Nicole Goosby

TRAPHOUSE KING **I II & III**

KINGPIN KILLAZ I II III

STREET KINGS

PAID IN BLOOD

By **Hood Rich**

LIPSTICK KILLAH **I, II, III**

Jibril Williams

CRIME OF PASSION I & II
By **Mimi**
STEADY MOBBN' **I, II, III**
By **Marcellus Allen**
WHO SHOT YA **I, II, III**
Renta
GORILLAZ IN THE BAY **I II**
DE'KARI
TRIGGADALE
Elijah R. Freeman
GOD BLESS THE TRAPPERS I, II, III
THESE SCANDALOUS STREETS I, II, III
FEAR MY GANGSTA I, II, III
THESE STREETS DON'T LOVE NOBODY I, II
BURY ME A G I, II, III, IV, V
A GANGSTA'S EMPIRE I, II, III, IV
Tranay Adams
THE STREETS ARE CALLING
Duquie Wilson
MARRIED TO A BOSS… I II
By Destiny Skai & Chris Green
KINGS OF THE GAME I II
Playa Ray
SLAUGHTER GANG II
By Willie Slaughter
THE HEART OF A SAVAGE
By Jibril Williams

BOOKS BY LDP'S CEO, CA$H

TRUST IN NO MAN

TRUST IN NO MAN 2

TRUST IN NO MAN 3

BONDED BY BLOOD

SHORTY GOT A THUG

THUGS CRY

THUGS CRY 2

THUGS CRY 3

TRUST NO BITCH

TRUST NO BITCH 2

TRUST NO BITCH 3

TIL MY CASKET DROPS

RESTRAINING ORDER

RESTRAINING ORDER 2

IN LOVE WITH A CONVICT

Coming Soon

BONDED BY BLOOD 2

BOW DOWN TO MY GANGSTA